"LET US BE FRANK. I HAVE NO INTEREST IN YOU OTHER THAN AS A BROOD MARE."

Colby wished that she could forget Lord Nevil's harsh declaration of heartless desire, but she could not—especially now, at this distinctly unmagical moment, as she faced him in their bedchamber.

In public, they pretended to be lovebirds. That was part of their agreement. But here in private, there would be no pretense of what their marriage was really about.

"We can postpone this night," he said, seeing the tremors running through her.

In answer, Colby took a glass of brandy and downed it in a gulp. "Unpleasantness postponed is still unpleasantness," she declared, set the empty glass down, went to the bed, and climbed into it.

After all, she told herself, she had no cause to complain. This was the bargain she had made, and she would not back down from it, no matter what it cost her in pride and pain.

But at the first touch of Nevil's lips on hers, and his first superbly skilled caress, Colby began to suspect that what was to come was far more than she had bargained for

The Divi

D1714254

THE
DIVIDED
HEART

by

Marcy Elias Rothman

A SIGNET BOOK

SIGNET
Published by the Penguin Group
Penguin Books USA Inc., 375 Hudson Street,
New York, New York 10014, U.S.A.
Penguin Books Ltd, 27 Wrights Lane,
London W8 5TZ, England
Penguin Books Australia Ltd, Ringwood,
Victoria, Australia
Penguin Books Canada Ltd, 10 Alcorn Avenue,
Toronto, Ontario, Canada M4V 3B2
Penguin Books (N.Z.) Ltd, 182–190 Wairau Road,
Auckland 10, New Zealand

Penguin Books Ltd, Registered Offices:
Harmondsworth, Middlesex, England

First published by Signet,
an imprint of Dutton Signet,
a division of Penguin Books USA Inc.

First Printing, September, 1994
10 9 8 7 6 5 4 3 2 1

*In memory
of
David Paul Elias,
Max Allan Elias,
My beloved big brothers,
and the best of men.*

Prologue

Lady Colby Mannering galloped into Moreton as if the Furies were chasing her.

They were.

Dark hair flying like a pennant behind her small brimmed hat, the black riding costume flaring around her, dark eyes on fire, she was a sight to halt the frantic traffic of farmers readying their wares for market day.

If the way she arrived, if the fantastic picture she made—tall and straight, riding her horse like a man—weren't enough to make her the cynosure of all eyes, Lady Colby was brandishing a whip in a way which left no doubt she knew how to use it.

Town and farm women stared in shock, while men's eyes riveted on the demon spectacle before them.

"What is she about now?" an old farmer asked of no one. It was a rhetorical question anyway.

Lady Colby rode straight for the sheep pens and stopped abruptly as her horse stood dancing on hind legs. She searched the crowd gathered outside until her eyes found and held a fat, foppish figure in gaiters and riding jacket, a bald, red-faced man in his late fifties.

"Panaman," Lady Colby shouted over the din of sheep, auctioneers, and farmers dickering among themselves.

The man called Panaman turned.

"I call you a whoremaster and defiler," Lady Colby shouted, driving her horse sideways, forcing a path.

The crowd parted in silence, leaving Panaman exposed.

Lady Colby flicked the end of the whip like a master, forcing the man to dance like a dervish on hot coals.

"You'll not fornicate among my people," she shouted, and this time she laid on the whip until Augustus Panaman cried for mercy.

Chapter 1

"You've just won a fortune, and you look like death warmed over," Sir Robert Morton laughed, studying his uncle. "How can you be blue-deviled after such an afternoon?"

Lord Nevil Browning reared back as if struck and made to leave the crowded parlor of an inn near Colchester, where many of his London friends who had lost and won fortunes were delighted to talk of the mill that went fifty rounds. He turned back and clapped his nephew and heir on the shoulder with false bonhomie.

Indeed, what is wrong with me, Nevil Browning asked himself? Why can three thousand men witness the same mill in hysterical rapture, one that will go down in boxing history for sheer brutality, and I come away with a sour taste and a blinding headache for all the gold in my pocket?

"I say, you're not becoming a prig, are you?" his nephew asked good-humoredly. Actually, the younger man's innocent question covered a growing world of concern. They were the best of friends as well as relations, but lately Sir Robert had become increasingly alarmed by his uncle's mercurial humors. Often the young man noticed that Nevil seemed to retreat into himself in ways that were so unlike him. The heart and soul of a party, the Nonpareil of Nonpareils, adored by every woman under eighty, and for all his open disdain and cold pride, the envy of every man aspiring to be a leader of the *ton*.

"Really, Robert, you are a fool," Nevil said after a while, returning to his table. The last thing Nevil wanted was to have his private demons exposed for all to see. It was enough he had to live with them. He was not a man to think that a burden shared was a burden halved. Never had and never would.

Some of the revelers came to their table to talk to Robert, and the interruption gave Nevil time to think about the cloud that seemed to hang over him more and more lately. Of course, he told himself, he knew the genesis of this day's displeasure. The brutal, senseless fight brought too many reminders of the blood, gore, and savagery of Badajoz. Nevil shook himself. This was not the place or time for such dangerous musings.

He was almost glad when Sir Jeffrey Coon, his young cousin, came reeling up to them after Robert's friends departed. Nevil was shocked by the changes he saw in the boy. At twenty, soured and debauched by too much riotous living, Jeffrey was drunk and disheveled and nearly fell over their table.

"Hear you two made a packet," Coon sneered, pushing Robert's steadying hand away. "Too damned lucky by half."

"Your luck's been out a good deal lately, I hear," Robert said, unable to hide his glee at the other's misfortunes.

Jeffrey swore and attempted to grab for Robert's throat. Nevil had to move quickly to separate them.

"I can't stand this childish nonsense between you two," Nevil whispered angrily. "There will be more than enough money and land when I die."

Jeffrey Coon muttered a string of curses and careened off.

"Please don't talk like that, Uncle Nev," Robert said. "It's not money. Jeff can't abide being second in anything."

Nevil was instantly struck by his nephew's perception.

"He feels cut out and hates the way you've taken me under your protection."

"By God, I'll never worry about you again," Nevil said.

Restored at once to good humor, Nevil took a full decanter from a passing waiter and leapt on the table. Tall and broad-shouldered, he loomed over the crowd, which egged him on. When he'd emptied the bottle, he called out, "Drinks for the house, landlord."

The room went wild in appreciation of the man who was their leader in every adventure his nimble mind could devise. They would follow him into any foolhardy hell and scrape, and had done this so often that Browning had become a legend to the *ton* for eight years past.

Chapter 2

Lady Colby Mannering arrived in London in no mood for the jollities and pleasures of the capital, even when a pedantic schoolmaster on the coach insisted on pointing them out to her. She had even less appreciation for the unabashed admiration of the layabouts at the inn where the coach deposited her.

Of course, she knew she was fair game traveling without an abigail, that oh-so-necessary appendage to a woman alone in London. But a maid, at this stage of her life, if not forever, must be foregone. It did not faze her for a moment.

Taking a box of books and her portmanteau, she fended off offers of assistance in such a determined way as to make her intentions crystal clear, and the hangers-on fell back. Head high, she walked for a few blocks at a strong pace until a handsome older man came toward her.

"Could you tell me how to get to Lincoln's Inn?" Colby inquired politely.

The man smiled and pointed Colby north with explicit directions, of which she only remembered Gray's Inn Road and Holborn.

Later, when the bags began to weigh heavily and forced her to slow her pace, Colby regretted her decision not to take a cab. Her thin store of money did not run to extravagance, and walking suited her. Colby scolded herself in the same tone she used toward her two young brothers. That made her smile, and she resumed her normally long stride, telling herself the bags were really not at all heavy.

At last she arrived at Chancery Lane and knew she was near

her destination. After a few wrong turns, she finally arrived at Avery Meredith's crowded bookstore, which was hidden in an obscure arcade.

Although she had never seen the bookseller, she had known his name and reputation for years. Only a few weeks before, when she was cleaning out the last of her father's papers, she came upon a packet of correspondence dating back forty years. In point of fact, it was partly because of that discovery, as well as other more vexing matters, that Colby was in London at a time when she could ill afford the luxury of travel.

She reminded herself that reverie was a waste of time, and with more vigor than she intended, pushed open the paned door of the bow-fronted shop.

The sight of the tall, elegant figure made the owner's heart turn over. With eyes the color of amethyst mixed with sapphires and skin so flawless it would have strained the pen of Shakespeare, she was a sight to make a man forget the pains and aches of age.

"May I help you?" the old man asked kindly in a dusty, cracked voice.

"Mr. Avery Meredith?"

The man nodded.

"I am Lady Colby Mannering. My father . . ."

"Colonel Mannering. I should say Lord Aden Mannering," the old man corrected himself. "I read of his death in the *Times*, of course. My sincerest condolences."

Colby curbed her impatience while the man talked of his regard for her father.

"A poet, a scholar," Mr. Meredith said. "What a waste it was when his family forced him into the army."

You don't know the half of what his family did to him, Colby thought. But this was not the time to lament that gentle giant, the perfect square peg in a round hole. She regretted once again that she had not been able to mourn him as he deserved.

"So kind of you to remember him," Colby said, girding her courage for the business at hand. "I wonder if you would look at these, sir."

Meredith took the book bag from her and, with the special

reverence book lovers reserve for literary rarities, exclaimed over the old volumes.

"They are treasures, my dear. Treasures."

"Are they valuable then?"

"You wish to sell these?" The man went white, as if she'd told him she wanted to sell a well-loved child. Book people were like that, she knew. Books were as precious to them as kin. She hadn't been the daughter of such a man as Aden Mannering for twenty-four years without understanding his and Mr. Meredith's awe of the written word.

Still the question of selling the books hung in the air like an accusation, and Colby wavered. The realities of the world outside this sheltered, musty realm of books and things of the mind soon intruded.

"I have no choice but to sell them for as much money as I can."

The old man looked at the handsome young woman before him, so much like her sainted father, a cherished client for more years than he could remember. Their correspondence from all over the world traced the soldier-scholar's career, especially the long years of service in India. The bookseller smiled.

"I am not a rich man, my lady, but perhaps . . ."

Colby cut him off in midsentence.

"You are too kind, but I cannot permit that," Colby said, her deep, musical voice catching on the words. "I want only a fair price."

The man understood at once. Colby Mannering was proud and purse poor, a lethal combination. She was a member of a very special breed. He often had to deal with people who had come down in the world. It was never a pleasant task.

He hastened to the small wooden cage at the side of the store. "Permit me to give you a receipt and a small payment, until I can find someone who will value these books as your father did."

In short order the book dealer handed Colby a piece of paper and a wad of bills. Colby was stunned. She wanted to, but couldn't allow herself to count the money. It was too shaming to show her need. She had never expected so much, and the dealer had said this was only a fraction of what he hoped to receive for the books in the end.

"You are too generous," she protested lamely.

"Lady Colby, you really must not say that," Meredith laughed. "When one is doing business, one is always supposed to be wary of being robbed. That is at least what my wife tells me."

Colby smiled, trying to hold back tears of relief. After all she had been through since her father's sudden death the year before, Mr. Meredith's kindness was the first consideration of any sort she had known. Her neighbors had studiously avoided her after the funeral. They all knew the sorry state of the Mannering's finances, and were clearly afraid bad luck was contagious, she reflected bitterly.

"I shall never forget you, Mr. Meredith," Colby said, bending to kiss the old man on his weathered cheek.

He held his hand against the spot where Colby had kissed him long after she left the shop.

Colby wandered in a daze before asking directions to Covent Garden. Walking at a pace that did not allow her to see any of the comings and goings of the most exciting city in the world, she was afraid to hope that her successful meeting with the bookseller would augur well for her next two interviews. She needed all the luck she could get.

Colby shuddered at the difficult prospects ahead of her. Life had made her a realist and old beyond her years. She quickened her pace. Self-pity was not her strong suit.

Normally a free spirit, Colby would do anything to amuse and divert her admiring brothers in an effort to make up for their father's gentle neglect and her mother's long absences. But last year had been a nightmare, ever since her father had been forced to confess the true state of the family's finances. From a carefree hoyden, she had become dour and old beyond her years.

Colby was glad to be able to turn her mind away from her gloomy musings, when she suddenly came upon the marvelous John Nash colonnade done in the Doric style built to surround the Opera House. She knew that at No. 2 she'd find Johnson

and Justerini, the wine and spirit merchants who had served
the Mannering family for generations.

She straightened her shoulders and prayed that her saucy
bonnet and pretty pelisse looked as good on her at it had on
her mother. Colby's tastes ran to riding clothes and hard,
curly-brimmed hats, but when necessary to be feminine, as it
was now, she knew how to carry off matters in style. She took
a deep breath and headed straight for the wineshop.

She needn't have worried about the impression she would
make. Two young shop assistants were eager to serve her until
one of the partners elbowed them off. Colby smiled beguil-
ingly, and soon the man was ushering her into his office. The
name Mannering and her willowy figure accorded her the attention she hoped would be profitable as well.

Chapter 3

"Cortnage, you are threatening my good nature," Lord Nevil said negligently.

Harvey Cortnage, the Browning family man of business, cringed.

"You should know better than to show your face this early in the morning. I will have my secretary's ears for allowing you above stairs," Browning went on, warming to the upheaval he was causing in his all-male household.

Nevil Morton William Matthew Wilson, eighth Lord Browning, was suffering from the greatest hangover in an eight-year history of the ubiquitous malady. His nerves, he decided, were steel rods making monstrous sounds in the cotton wool that was his brain. He was certain his eyes were glued together across the bridge of what he knew some called his too-aristocratic nose. His mouth had surely been used by the Horse Guards for a battle, leaving each tooth a leaning tower of Pisa, testament to a resounding defeat.

While he was taking stock of his condition, his secretary, John Lear, slipped quietly into the room. Studying Lord Browning in the throes of a sore head, Lear, the most patient of men, could only marvel at his employer's suffering, and at last found it in his heart to rescue Cortnage. He steered the fat little man firmly by the elbow out of the room and down the magnificent winged stairs.

"Really, sir, I tried to warn you about his lordship's head, but you would have it your own and—as you just saw—almost disastrous way," John chided Cortnage.

"That's all well and good, but sometimes he must think

about other matters besides mills and drink. His estate manager at Moreton has been . . . "

John Lear interrupted out of loyalty to his master, and was not about to give the punctilious toady satisfaction of any kind. His affection for Lord Nevil was the motif pin of his life, even if he could not like all of his employer's rakehell doings.

"I suggest, Mr. Cortnage, that you write him a very strong letter of particulars, and let me broach it to his lordship when the moment is right."

The secretary ushered the man out the front door, but not before he saw the most striking woman across the way. He was sure she was looking straight at him, and felt the most compelling need to adjust his muslin neckcloth. I needn't have bothered, Lear sighed, when the lady hastened off at the very sight of him.

Lady Colby Mannering was on her second round of the square, where Lord Browning's large, white mansion dwarfed all the other Georgian houses flanking it. Colby felt her fabled courage desert her again just when she needed it most. She no longer felt the coolheaded firebrand she knew her neighbors called her. The task she had set herself had seemed impossible when it first occurred to her several days before, and now it seemed absurd. Yet she knew she had nowhere else to turn.

Colby passed the house, her hands damp within the thin lilac kid gloves she wore, her stomach empty and knotted. She would have given anything for a restorative cup of tea and a biscuit. She had not eaten for hours.

"The world hates a coward," echoed through her head. The old family adage that had lightened her life many times came to Colby unbidden.

When for the third time she started to shy away, Colby remembered that her day had started splendidly with the bookseller and wine merchant eager to assist her. The gentlemanly wine dealer had found it hard to believe that the cellars at Brawleigh still contained pipes of brandy and port laid down by her great-grandfather on his coming of age.

How this small gold mine of the vintner's art had eluded her spendthrift grandfather's and uncles' prodigious appetites was a minor miracle in itself. The wine merchant said the samples she'd brought were first rate.

Often, while she was growing up in India, her father would put her to sleep talking of England, his beloved Brawleigh Manor, her grandfather and uncles.

Aden Mannering, despairing of ever having sons before the boys were born, had treated Colby as an equal. To satisfy her endless questions about England, he would tell her stories about his family's exploits in London. He did not disguise their peccadillos. Soon Colby knew that in their profligacy the three men were as different from her father as chalk from cheese. That her father had missed the family's predilection for high living was a mystery even Aden Mannering could never explain. Her grandfather and her uncles were legendary topers, sportsmen, bad gamblers, and fools for the hearts and favors of expensive women, while her father was a man of the mind. She loved him for it and missed him sorely.

Pleased that some of the great vintages had survived consumption, Colby knew that whatever she profited from them would mean the merest drop in the proverbial bucket. Still, she could not help wondering what other great assets the family had sold and squandered that might have been preserved for her brothers' future. What she needed, as everyone was quick to tell her, was a fortune, and she needed it immediately.

With no other way out of her dilemma, she crossed the road and approached the black door with the magnificent fanlight. Colby quickly lifted the huge door knocker, with the face of a ferocious lion, and let it fall. She heard the sound resound in the hallway beyond. Her heart beating wildly, her mouth dry as the Sahara, she waited.

The door was opened by the largest and most imposing man, more grand than any bishop, she had ever seen, she thought. Tall as she was, Colby had to crane her neck painfully to see his face. With a doleful face and manner, he waited for her to state her business.

"I am the Lady Colby Mannering, and I wish an interview with Lord Nevil Browning at once," she said, putting on the airs and graces she knew snobs relished and expected from the Quality. She was good at that sort of thing, the result of years

of depressing the overtures of ambitious subalterns in her father's regiment. She sensed that the butler was arguing with
himself before replying.

"It is the most inopportune moment, my lady," he said at
last. "If you will wait, I shall ask Lord Nevil's secretary if he
can see you."

He ushered her into a side room off the grand, soaring entry
hall.

The butler knocked timidly and threw open the library door.

"Mr. Lear, sir, there is a lady awaiting speech with his lordship."

"Are you out of your mind, Balcomb," Lear bellowed, his
normal placidity giving way to anger. "He'll flay us alive."

"Flay who alive?" Before either could move, Colby was in
the room.

Balcomb was astonished, but recovered enough to leave the
matter in Lear's hands. The secretary was thunderstruck, rec-
ognizing Colby as the woman he had seen across the road.

"I am afraid, Madam . . ."

"Lady Colby Mannering," she said sweetly.

She could see that her title didn't change matters. Colby
liked that, and he was at once raised five notches in her acute
and often critical evaluation of men.

"I waited as late as I dared to call upon his lordship this
morning, but I must see him at once."

Lear was bowled over by her dark, sparkling eyes and skin
to rival the most prized ivory, and it took him seconds before
he could recover his wit. John Lear hated being the one chosen
to send away Lord Browning's conquests, some real, but many
imagined. A smile, a polite word was enough to make many
women feel they had attained Nirvana, and that Lord Nevil desired them above all others. They were almost always wrong.
In his way, Nevil Browning was a loyal man, and his true
lights o' love could be sure he dealt in one woman at a time. It
could not be said of many of his friends.

But Lear, whose experience of women was, for the most
part, secondhand, knew none of this applied to Lady Colby.
But it was worth his job, if not his life, to avoid plaguing his
employer and mentor too far at any time.

"I fear, madam, you have chosen the most inappropriate hour," he said. "May I suggest another day when he is feeling more the thing."

Colby tried to hide her distress.

"I wish I could say I had another time to speak with Lord Nevil, but I am in London only until tomorrow, and my business is a matter of great urgency," she said, more wistfully than she meant. "I am his neighbor in Moreton, you see. Perhaps that might carry some weight."

Neighbor or no neighbor, Lear was sure it would mean nothing to his employer. But something in the woman—her dignity, her quiet command, the effort to control whatever was disturbing her—reached out to him, and he decided to risk his lordship's ill humor nonetheless. He offered Colby a chair and left the room to announce Colby Mannering's arrival.

"Can't you see I am in no condition to receive anyone," Nevil Browning protested between sips from a huge cup of coffee his valet had to hold for him.

Lear laughed in spite of himself and mimicked the state of his employer's head.

"You'll pardon me, sir, but were you one of the combatants at the mill? The loser perhaps?"

"You are very daring today, John," his lordship observed dryly while his valet helped him into a coat that could only have been sculpted over his chest and shoulders by a master tailor.

"I say, sir, she really has no other time to see you, and I thought perhaps you could spare Lady Colby, who is, after all, your neighbor . . ."

"Mannering. That sounds familiar," Nevil said, "but there weren't any women. Two brothers died without issue, I think. Perhaps it's the wife of the one who went to India."

The idea that Lady Colby might be married had never entered Lear's head. Somehow she didn't look married. Nothing about her suggested it, and he felt a sense of bitter disillusionment at the possibility. What a fool I am. She is far above my touch, he thought, remembering that a man with his few prospects must not have dreams of anyone remotely like Lady

Colby. As it was, he counted his blessings at the good fortune he had to attach himself to someone like Browning.

"Will you see her then?" Lear blurted out, throwing caution to the wind.

"Absolutely not," Nevil said, effectively sending him away with a flea in his ear. "I'm in no fit condition for visitors, especially ladies."

With dragging steps, the young secretary returned to the book room.

"I am terribly sorry, my lady, but his lordship cannot see you. He is unwell," his disappointment for her evident and endearing.

I appreciate your help, Mr. . . . ?"

"John Lear."

Colby rose from her chair and began drawing on her gloves, moving toward the door.

"It troubles me that Lord Nevil will hear my news from others," she said, trying to hide her dismay. Her last chance for salvation was dashed. The panic she had been trying to keep in check threatened to burst out of her, and she began to tremble inside. What hurt most was that Colby knew she had been stupidly wicked to place so much faith in a meeting with Browning. He had been her last hope, and he wouldn't even give her the courtesy of a hearing.

John Lear could not know the source of her perturbation, but that she was in some kind of dire need was obvious, and his heart went out to her. He could not leave matters as they stood.

"May I take you to where you are staying?"

Colby nodded, unable to speak for the moment, and reached for the door. It swung open with sudden force, nearly knocking her off her feet.

"What the hell . . . ?"

Lord Nevil's obvious displeasure at finding her still in his house gave Colby the courage of desperation. Her fury at his high-handedness, forcing his secretary to lie for him when he was obviously well enough to be dressed to go out, his relegating her to a common nuisance, sent her temper, not the best of her qualities, soaring.

"Mr. Lear, excuse us," Colby said between clenched teeth and held the door open for him.

Nevil was speechless.

Colby closed the door and turned to him.

"I came here to offer to have your child!"

Chapter 4

"You're mad." Browning was sure his hearing was playing him up and retreated further toward the door, his considerable courage shaken.

Colby stood her ground while he looked at her through bloodshot eyes, not at all sure she wasn't a raving maniac.

"Hear me out," she said with patient resignation, as if he were an idiot child. "I am making you a perfect proposal. I will raise the child in the country, stay out of your path in every way, manage your estate and mine, all while you continue to live the bachelor life you obviously like so much. And all you can do is send me away like some importunate beggar."

"And why should I marry you of all people?" Nevil asked incredulously, eyeing her up and down. "I can have my pick of any woman I want in London."

Stung as much by the blatant cruelty as the justice of what Lord Browning was saying, Colby felt the fire within her falter and longed to run and hide from the shame that swept over her like a fever. Painful as it was, she had to ask herself what else should she have expected from a man who was spoiled rotten from birth, protected by enormous wealth, the only son of elderly, doting parents, with the appearance of an Olympian God? What can Nevil "Bleeding" Browning know of the realities of the world beyond the battlements of privilege, Colby asked herself bitterly.

Nevil was contending with the twin evils of a stomach in revolt against gravity and the unmistakable hurt his unchecked words had caused. For a precious second he thought to apologize for his breach of good manners, but she seemed to recover too quickly for any lasting damage, he was glad to see. She was not a woman, he noted, easily daunted.

He was wrong. Colby walked across the book room to the fireplace, her back turned so that she could take command of herself again. She had to make one last appeal whatever the cost to her self-respect.

"Really, my lord, I am not raving, though I can see where you might have reason to think so," she said, trying a new, softer tack. "I don't want to be married to you any more than you want to marry me, or have your child or any man's. But I needed to command your attention."

"You have succeeded," Browning replied grudgingly. "I will give you one minute more, madam, to state your case."

"My father died almost a year ago, the estate is bankrupt, and I must restore it to give my brothers, my mother, and my aunt a roof over their heads," Colby said, hurrying on before Browning could flee.

"I'm sorry about your father, but why come to me?" he asked, still at a loss.

"I need you to help me secure a loan to pay off my most pressing creditors and allow us to get on with our lives."

"Go to a bank," Nevil said, edging toward the door.

"Have you ever gone to a bank?" Colby asked, her voice liquid acid. "Bankers love Brownings. They help people who don't need them. It is bad enough the estate is insolvent, they have told me they don't trust a woman to bring Brawleigh back to life."

"And I heartily agree with them," Nevil said, extracting a half-hunter from his coat pocket.

"I am sorry for you," Browning added, opening the door to find Lear and Balcomb, pale and trembling without. "But I cannot cure all the ills of the world."

Browning began his escape.

"I think before you dismiss me, my lord, you should know that I horsewhipped your estate manager in full view of Moreton's citizenry."

"I knew you were a menace." Browning was stunned.

"He raped a fourteen-year-old maid, who committed suicide

in my kitchen," Colby threw back at him. "You might do your own dirty work and pay some attention to your tenants and those who oversee them in your high-and-mighty name."

With her considerable dignity in full sail, Colby left the room.

Chapter 5

Nevil Browning found himself thinking about his visitor more than he wanted. The interview with the lady had left him shaken, almost as much as his weekend revels.

His head throbbed and his eyes burned in the cool sunlight of a late November day. His body, once lithe and quick to respond to his commands, felt like an oxcart on a rutted lane. It was a measure of his state that he had dismissed his groom and sent his horse back to the stables in the mews, hoping that a brisk walk would restore some semblance of his usual vigor. It was a mistake, he knew now. He might not die of his hangover, although he devoutly wished otherwise.

Once free of his house and the less than approving glances of his staff, he couldn't decide where to make his first stop of the day. He had a meeting at his club, but that was later. Unused to wondering what to do with himself, and very much suffering from lowered spirits after his most unsatisfactory encounter with the Lady Colby, he found himself wandering aimlessly.

Soon he knew that his conscience, an unsympathetic organ that frequently gave Nevil problems, was not about to give him much peace.

He saw again the way his unkind words—true as they might be—had sent Lady Colby reeling. He cursed himself for appearing the very kind of supercilious Bond Street beau he hated most in the world, the sort of man whose whole life was pleasure, a preening, overweening, self-centered peacock with too much time, too much money, and too much air between the ears to care about anything more than his own appetites.

Besides the thought that he might indeed become the kind of mindless man of the *ton* he abhorred, Nevil's great nightmare was that he might one day end up as so many of his sporting friends. They were wed to impeccably proper and pedigreed females paraded on the Marriage Market like so much prime cattle each year. Bowled over by their fresh charms and clinging ways, his friends fell out of love by the end of the honeymoon or soon after as made no difference.

Thank God for Robert, Browning told himself, and smiled with pleasure. The boy was all any man could wish for in an heir, if, like himself, one had no desire for marriage and a string of puling and puking brats of his own. Orphaned when his father died in the Peninsular and his mother soon after of a broken heart, Robert fell under the care of Nevil and his mother, and a happier family trio never was.

Thinking of his nephew reminded Nevil that he had to do something about Jeffrey Coon. Browning knew the bad blood between the two young men was a reflection of the hatred between his mother, Lady Miriam, and the boy's grandmother. They were sisters-in-law who had never got on and who fanned the animosity between their only grandsons. It was a small family, and Nevil always felt the feud was an unseemly display of greed and jealousy over trivialities.

Thoughts of ancient family history reanimated Nevil's aching head, and he strode with some purpose toward his mother's house. She had been away, and he missed her sorely, an admission he would make to no one, not even Lady Miriam herself.

As he rounded into her street just off Hyde Park, he saw a gathering of Bow Street runners and a crowd of onlookers.

Chapter 6

Colby Mannering took the few steps to the small entry of Belden's Hotel, dragging each foot as if manacled to the ground. Her weariness was so palpable that the manageress's heart ached for her guest.

"May I send up some tea and toast, my lady?" Mrs. Bolton asked kindly.

"Yes, please." Colby smiled shyly, touched by the older woman's care, and proceeded up the stairs to her room.

Colby undressed and put on her father's old brocaded robe and lay down on the bed to think of her next move. She tried to calm her shaking limbs, rubbing her hands up and down her arms to bring some warmth to her body.

She was bereft of hope and angry with herself for having so little to recommend her to the towering ice man, for whom talk of money, especially the lack of it, could only be construed as the worst sort of social breach.

Colby was disgusted with herself for being so naive as to think that she could appeal to Nevil Browning for assistance. His cold exterior and his neglect of Moreton House that stood sentinel over the marvelous estate that marched with Brawleigh was legendary. And even worse was the ugly way he permitted Augustus Panaman to run the place like a medieval fiefdom, having his way with every woman and girl his greedy little eyes alighted on.

Immediately she was reminded of poor Ida Hooper, the pretty daughter of her own gardener, who killed herself rather than submit to the estate manager again. In a way, her shock and pity for the girl was why she was in London on a trip she now knew was an unmitigated disaster.

Two nights earlier Colby had been in the library late into the night, again going over ledgers trying to find ways to save her brothers' future, when her Aunt Sylvia had come in crying with a terrible story.

"Come to the kitchen at once," her aunt had pleaded. "The Hooper girl is hanging in our larder."

Colby found her household wringing their hands in hysterics. When no one would assist her, Colby cut the girl down and, in her take-charge manner, made arrangements for a decent burial.

The tragic suicide made her determine to put a halt to Panaman's unchecked reign of terror throughout the neighborhood. It was then she decided on the public horsewhipping, which brought forth other tales of the man's treacheries. He was known to require anyone doing business with Moreton House to pay him tribute and to have tyrannized the tenants in every way possible.

Her first thought had been to write to Browning and tell him of Panaman's cruelties. Better still, she had decided she would propose to take over the management of Moreton in return for help in setting Brawleigh to rights.

The thought of offering to have his child, which now made her blush in shame, came to her in the quiet of her bedroom the morning before she left for London. She knew at the time it was indeed madness to have even thought of it, but she had rehearsed the scene in her own mind and saw it as a way of propelling him into listening to her. Surprise, her father had told her, was a very effective weapon in war. Wasn't saving her family a war?

But all that was past history. At once the memory of how Browning looked her up and down and found her beneath his touch could no longer be denied. All the way home with John Lear at her side exchanging the rankest inanities, she had barely been able to hold back the picture of her encounter with Browning, afraid to look at it for what it was . . . devastation.

With a few neatly delivered home truths, Nevil Browning had ripped her up one side and down the other, as only a Regency Buck of the first rank knew how to do. She had heard that they often made great sport of depressing the pretensions, dreams, and hopes of women hanging out for eligible husbands. A special victim were women with pockets to let, as Colby's were. And a family ruined by excesses was certainly not attractive, she told herself.

Nevil had found her wanting on every level, and had left her as profoundly shattered as if he had taken a mallet to a crystal vase. That was the image that came to her, and all at once Colby knew what real hatred could be. Her breath came sharp and hard, making her shake uncontrollably.

He'll pay for this, Colby promised. And when honesty forced her to laugh at the emptiness of the threat, she doubled her fists and pounded on the narrow bed until bitter tears coursed down her face.

With her face buried in the coverlet, Colby did not hear the light knock or the door open.

"I've taken the liberty of adding a boiled egg and a glass of Madeira, my lady," the manageress said, making her presence known. She placed a tray on a table, tactfully allowing Colby to dry her tears and tidy her hair.

"How lovely," Colby told her and pretended to enjoy the small repast while Mrs. Bolton hovered. She wasn't in the least hungry, but she didn't want to appear unmindful of the woman's generosity.

Colby could tell that Mrs. Bolton wanted to talk and, as much as she wanted a sympathetic ear, she was unable to do more than smile. Shy of sharing her stupid conduct, Colby wanted nothing more than to be alone. Her pride would not allow her to admit to anyone that her world was falling to pieces. Mrs. Bolton departed, and Colby left the remains on the tray and prowled the room, more alone than ever. She needed to plan her next move, knowing there were few, if any, alternatives open to her now that Browning had refused to help her.

Tomorrow, before she left London, she would have to see her father's man of business and tell him to find a buyer for the estate. Although, with all the mortgages on it, she knew they would be lucky to come away with little more than the clothes they stood in.

Colby reached for the glass of wine on the tray, downed it in a gulp, and went to dress. What she needed was air and movement. I won't come down with the megrims. That's my mother's province, she told herself sternly and quitted the room in a rush.

She walked for hours in numbing cold trying to sort out her future, her head whirling from one dead end to another.

The idea of poverty didn't frighten Colby for herself. She might not like it, but she knew she would get on somehow. But she minded very much that her young brothers, Matthew and Mark, would have to make their own way in the world without money or influence to smooth the road. The boys were the last of the Mannering line, and the title was the only asset the family had remaining. At the moment it was worse than nothing.

As for her mother and her aunt, that was another matter. Her aunt would cope, as she had done for so many years, always in the shadow of her older sister, Phillida, Colby's mother. The one small, dumpy, and kindhearted, the placid professional spinster; the other tall, disdainful, the black-haired reigning beauty. In her own mind, at least, Lady Phillida had always felt herself deserving of more than a colonial existence in India as the wife of an unambitious, introverted scholar.

At seven o'clock, Colby dragged herself up the hotel steps, in no way restored in heart or mind.

Chapter 7

Nevil's heart stopped at the sight of Dr. Eliot Corday, the family physician, who was plunging into the crowd in front of his mother's house, trying to force a way to his carriage. As the two locked eyes, Corday retreated into the house with Nevil at his heels. Just inside, Nevil grabbed the older man's arm.

"Mother?"

"Robert." The doctor turned and led the way to the book room. "I'm most awfully sorry."

John Lear met them at the door. Nevil saw at once that his massive desk had been cleared and made into a makeshift bier. On it lay Robert Morton, his face white and stony, much like the carved images of young crusaders he'd seen in village churches up and down the length of England. Nevil fell heavily into a large, brocaded chair nearby.

John appeared at his elbow and forced a heavily etched brandy glass into his hand. Nevil looked at it dumbly, almost as if he didn't know what it was.

"My poor mother," Nevil said, his voice thick.

"I've given her a sleeping draught," Dr. Corday said quickly.

Nevil nodded in approval, drank the brandy in a swallow, and handed the empty glass to Lear to refill.

The secretary took it, noticing his employer's hand shaking as if with ague.

"He didn't suffer," Corday said from the shadows of the large room. "Of that I am sure. It was a clean thrust to the heart."

"How did it happen?"

"Brigands waylaid Robert and two friends near the inn last evening returning from a party," Lear volunteered slowly. "Only Sir Robert resisted."

"The others?"

"Rigby Taylor and James Laughton-Muir, my lord," Corday interposed. "Slight wounds. I've seen them. They and their servants brought Robert here an hour ago."

"Dr. Corday summoned me," Lear added. "I went to your club, but you hadn't been there."

Browning rose to his feet and motioned Lear to join him at the desk.

"John, I want you to see this letter is delivered at once to Captain Tarn Maitland."

Dr. Corday, a tall, handsome man, graying at the temples, came forward and took Nevil's hand in silent condolence and began to leave the room. Lear took up paper and pen, waiting for Browning's dictation.

"My nephew Robert Morton was murdered in an encounter with highwaymen near the Hanging Man in Essex last evening," Nevil recited in a dead monotone, so unlike the rumbling voice John knew so well. "I would deem it a deep personal service if you could detach one of the Maitland Marines to look into the matter with all due haste. You must know I will not rest until I know the name of his killers."

The last was delivered in an even more sepulchral voice. It sent chills through Lear and Dr. Corday, who had remained transfixed at the door. Both men knew what Nevil Browning was about.

Like everyone else, the men knew Tarn Maitland's reputation. He was a towering, dark-haired, onyx-eyed figure known throughout London as Captain Black and White for the way he dressed, the horse and carriages he drove, and the livery worn by his servants and employees. Midas-rich, he was a formidable city entrepreneur turned member of Parliament, who in recent years had become a figure to be reckoned with in the hushed corridors of Whitehall. As for his Marines, they were a legendary force of men some called the Robin Hoods of London, who often went about redressing evils and sins in defense of the defenseless. In many ways they were an unofficial adjunct to the Bow Street runners. Corday and Lear knew if anyone could find and punish Robert Morton's slayers within the law, Maitland could be relied upon to do so.

"Are you sure you want to know who was behind this, my lord?" Corday dared to ask.

"You suspect Jeffrey Coon, as I do?"

The doctor nodded.

"God help him if he is," Lord Nevil replied, confirming for Corday and Lear the name of the man who most stood to gain by the death of Robert Morton.

Chapter 8

Colby Mannering waved the farmer a fond goodbye, took the shabby portmanteau from him, and trod the rutty avenue up to Brawleigh Hall.

The trip back from London in a heavy rain had been the devil's own nightmare. Deposited three miles from Moreton on the post road, she had been fortunate to find a ride with a man coming from the opposite direction who would pass the estate on his way home.

He was a dour, taciturn farmer, and that suited Colby. Her mind was in turmoil from all that had transpired between her disastrous meetings with Nevil Browning and her solicitor. The man had confirmed that Brawleigh was lost forever and that they would depart the house and land that had been in the family for two hundred years with virtually nothing.

Head down and bitter tears stinging her lids, she wasn't aware that her brothers and aunt were running down to meet her until Mark threw himself headlong into her arms, nearly sending her backward into the muddy road.

"What have you brought me?" Mark, the ten-year-old asked, seizing the bag she had dropped.

Colby was glad she had parted with a few shilling and bought the boys and her Aunt Sylvia innocent gifts. She consoled herself with the thought that a few moments of pleasure before she told them the awful truth of their future was worth the extravagance. There would be precious few pleasures in the foreseeable time ahead.

Matthew, solemn for his fourteen years, the picture of his father, accepted a slim book of poems and helped Colby with her portmanteau. With Mark clutching on to the wooden model of a horse, the two raced ahead, leaving Colby and her aunt to follow.

"No luck?" Sylvia Rainwriter asked. She was a tiny, bright-eyed woman who only wanted to enhance others. She lived in shadows of her own making and few knew her worth. Those who did, and Colby was chief among these, valued her wicked wit and quiet wisdom.

"Disaster. Just as you predicted."

Miss Rainwriter stopped abruptly and took Colby into her ample arms, and the two rocked in silent sympathy, two incongruous figures against the coming night and a winter storm to match the chill in their hearts.

"Will two hundred pounds help?" the older woman asked as they broke apart and resumed the walk to the house.

"Someone die and leave you a fortune?" Colby stopped and stared at her aunt.

"Might say that."

"Darling, no games, please. That kind of money won't save Brawleigh, but it could secure us a roof over our heads for a time."

"I had a beau once, and he left me something in his will," Sylvia said, proudly taking Colby's hand. "While you were away, I dug around in the attic and found the letter from his solicitor. I expected ten or twenty pounds, and he tells me it has grown to the grand sum of two hundred. It is yours."

Colby stood stock still, unable to move.

"Darling, I can't take that," she protested. "It's all you have in the world."

"You and the boys are all I want in the word," the older woman said emphatically.

"You didn't mention Mama," Colby observed wickedly.

"Speak of the devil," Miss Rainwater laughed. "She's back from Bath. The money you gave her has run out, and so has her welcome as an unpaying guest. Fate does not test us singly."

The two looked at each other and, despite the bleak clouds over their lives, they laughed until they cried, unaware that Augustus Panaman observed them through strong binoculars from a distant hill south of the hall.

Chapter 9

For the third evening in a row, Nevil Browning took dinner with his mother at her bedside. They were often silent affairs, a gulf of pain separating them. The butler arrived with a footman, and the half-eaten food was mercifully removed. Neither spoke until the servants departed.

"Is everything prepared for the funeral?" Lady Miriam asked at last.

"Tomorrow at noon, at St. Margaret's Westminster," Nevil answered, pouring himself a large whiskey. "Everyone will understand if you don't attend."

Lady Miriam looked up sharply and took his glass.

"I shall be there." Her voice, no more than a croak since her grandson's death, was loud and firm. It was like music to Nevil. More than anything about the loss of Robert was seeing the spirit he loved in her die with each passing hour.

A glorious, unpredictable woman who had set London on its ears forty years earlier, Miriam Browning had been in her day a robust, red-haired hellion up to every feat of courage and outrage, not unlike the reputation her son had earned for himself the past few years. Age may have dimmed her wildness, but not her flamboyance. Seeing her white-faced, sunken figure under the silken coverlet the last few days had almost brought Nevil to tears a dozen times.

He and his mother shared a devotion that was not of the common sort. They led their lives as they pleased, and the bond between them was greater for the freedom they gave one another and the care each took in the other's happiness.

They might disapprove of the excesses each was capable of,

but they knew they were necessary to fill whatever emptiness existed in their lives. Robert had made up for much of that void. But Nevil remained haunted by memories of a battle he could never talk about, and Lady Miriam could not overcome the loss of her beloved husband and daughter within a week of each other.

And now that Robert was dead, mother and son knew they had to remake their lives yet again. But could they go down to the depths once again?

Lady Miriam returned Nevil's glass and sank back against the pillows, the effort to recover some of her former fight quickly dissipating. The searing pain each felt was palpable and hung in the air of the lavender and gold room.

"Promise me something, Nevil."

He waited, hopeful it was something he could do to ease her misery.

"Jeffrey Coon will never inherit. I cannot abide the thought that he should succeed by Robert's death." All reserve gone, Lady Miriam collapsed against the pillows and wept convulsively.

"I promise," Nevil said quietly. He touched her hand and quickly left the room.

Chapter 10

Colby closed the door on two men and a woman and wan-dered heartsick back to the drawing room.

"I won't have those awful people in my home again," Lady Phillida Mannering intoned from the depths of a worn green velvet couch, a vial held high as she tried to perfume away the presence of the people who had just departed.

"May I remind you once again, Mama," Colby said with frayed patience, "this is not your house. It is Matthew's, or was his until ten minutes ago."

"You haven't sold it to those . . ." Words failed Lady Phill-ida, and she began to weep.

"No one else wanted Brawleigh in the dilapidated state it's in," Colby said, weary of trying to get her mother to under-stand the truth of their finances. Unable to bear more of Lady Phillida's keening, Colby fled to her bedroom. She tore into her armoire and took out an old pair of her father's army rid-ing breeches and a shirt. These were her usual attire when she strode around the estate, but today she wore them to begin the onerous task of clearing out the attics.

Hours later, her hair and hands grimy with the dirt of years of discarded possessions, Colby stood scanning documents and letters she had found in a brassbound trunk.

This was where Nevil Browning found her.

Against the wishes of Lady Phillida and Sylvia Rainwriter, Browning had insisted on seeing Colby at once, and here he was staring at her as she stood outlined against a dormer win-dow, lost to everything around her.

Shocked at seeing a woman in breeches for the first time in

his life, he didn't know where to look. He knew he should turn away and leave, but he couldn't. She was riveting, a tall, lithe figure, the rounded full breasts outlined beneath the open shirt as thin as a sheet from years of washing. Stirred in ways he didn't want, Nevil made to turn around and leave, knocking over a three-legged chair in his haste.

"What are you doing here?" Colby cried, appalled to be taken unawares.

"I want to talk to you," he said lamely, trying mightily to keep his eyes off the full view of her bosom and the slightly rounded belly below the rough twine that held up breeches much too large for her.

"You seem to have a genius for making me feel the fool," she blasted, pushing him aside as she strode out of the attics.

God knows what I must look like to this bloody-minded man, she muttered to herself, hurrying along the gloomy corridor and making for the stairs. The idea that she was running away like some schoolgirl made Colby even more angry, and she slackened her pace. But instead of going to her room to change as she planned, she continued down the stairs, breathing fire at herself for a momentary lapse into missishness and concern for Browning's sensibilities. She arrived breathless at the library, mercifully unoccupied at the moment.

Colby saw her father's humidor on the table, and with trembling fingers extracted the biggest cigar she could find. If he was shocked at her clothing, she meant to compound the sin. She lit the cigar and exhaled deeply, as Browning stood nonplussed in the doorway

For all his reputed sophistication, Nevil found it difficult to accept her in men's clothes, smoking a cigar as carelessly as any toff. This woman will likely drive me mad, he told himself, yet he hurried to get his mission accomplished before he lost his nerve.

"I am here to accept your offer of marriage . . ." he said, hating himself for stumbling over the words. He knew he could have been more tactful, but this woman set his teeth on edge and seemed to bring out the worst in him.

"Have all the women in London been struck deaf, dumb,

and blind at your entreaties?" she asked, her voice edged with unadulterated venom.

"Don't try me, Lady Mannering!"

"Don't expect me to swoon like some Rhine maiden, Lord Browning," she spat out. The scene of his turndown burned as brightly as the day it happened. "Remember you mortified me, knowing I made that preposterous proposal in desperation."

"I was unwell . . ."

"Drunk as a lord more like," she said, her voice crackling with fury. "But not reason enough to treat my feelings like dirt under your boot."

Colby stared blindly at him, wanting nothing more than to hurl the largest object she could find at his perfect head, covered, she noticed for the first time, in short, thick, blond curls as close as a cap, his eyes river blue. Furious at the turn her mind was taking, she studied the worn carpet while building the courage she needed.

"Out of this house, Lord Bloody Browning. It may not be ours for long, but, by God, while I am mistress here, I shall say who may enter and who may not."

Outraged, Nevil turned and left, but just beyond the library door, the bitter import of Colby Mannering's turndown forced him to turn back. He returned.

"If you change your mind, I shall be at Moreton House until dawn tomorrow."

She barely heard him, and when the door slammed shut, Colby's control evaporated and she slumped to the floor. Until she saw him again, Colby had not allowed herself to admit how much his brutal refusal had devastated her. Now overcome with the enormity of what she had done, years of holding every hurt and disappointment under her iron will thundered for release, and Colby let out a long, low animal lament. She buried her face in her arms and wept uncontrollably.

Nevil walked with dragging steps toward the stables, knowing at last the full meaning of the shame he had brought on her. He couldn't believe his cruelty. He quickened his step. Retrieving his horse, Nevil saw the Mannering boys wrestling in the unmown grass, their clothes as worn and patched as Colby's shirt, their shoes broken and poorly mended.

His mind went to the days when Robert had been a boy, and his sense of loss took his breath away.

Chapter 11

"Have you taken leave of your senses?" Lady Phillida Mannering screamed at her daughter. "Turning away Lord Nevil Browning's offer of marriage, all that money, the houses, the land, the position!"

Colby had just told her family what had happened between her and the handsome visitor in the afternoon. They were gathered in her mother's room, where she lay prostrate on her bed.

Aunt Sylvia, the soul of goodness and even temperament, had tried to calm her sister, warning that her great good looks would suffer if she continued. For a woman who had lived in the certain knowledge that her mirror never lied, it was an argument that normally curbed Lady Phillida's tempestuous nature, but not this day.

"You wicked, selfish girl," Phillida raged once again, her face mottled and ugly. "Worse, you're a fool just like your father. Never thinking of me, just himself."

"Phillida, that's enough," Miss Rainwriter said at last from the corner that was her accustomed place whenever voices were raised, usually at her sister's instigation. "What's done is done. Colby has her reasons."

"Reasons, ha."

"Mama, we'll come about. I promise you," Colby pleaded, more wretched than ever at what her unruly tongue, her desire to avenge herself on Nevil Browning had brought down on them all.

She saw her brothers huddled by the fire, their faces clouded with anxiety, their eyes swiveling from one adult to the other, unable to know what to make of their aunt, who never raised her voice above a whisper, and the sheer spite that sprung from their mother. Her outbursts when she was thwarted in any way always set the house on its ear.

All Colby could read from their silent appeal to her was that she was failing them. Her only concern for the past year was keeping the family together and the boys' lives on an even keel. She could do nothing to spare them the loss of their father, but she had tried to spare them the truth of their financial ruin, hoping for a miracle. The miracle had come, and she had thrown it away.

"Your high-and-mightiness has lost this house to those odious, nouveau riche, who behaved to me as if a perpetual stink were at the end of their noses," Lady Phillida took up her complaint once more. "And you dare send Lord Browning packing, when any sensible woman would have fainted at his feet. Shame on you."

Colby began to shepherd her brothers out of the room. They had heard enough for one night.

"No, let them hear," Lady Mannering thundered. "Let them know that I will never be able to show my head in society again now that everyone will know my freakish daughter turned down the most eligible parti in England. And what of my poor little boys, my poor old sister?"

Sylvia Rainwriter rose from her chair.

"You great fraud," she spat out in a voice none of them had ever heard before. "Now the truth comes out. When did you ever give a rap for your children, your husband, or me, for God's sake," she said, shaking in every limb. "You made poor Aden's life a misery, Colby a handmaiden, and a drudge out of me."

Overcome by her anger and the recital of truths she'd silently lived with for years, Sylvia stumbled from the room, her sobs of impotent rage stored up over a lifetime echoing in the hall.

While her daughter and sons reeled from the scene they'd just witnessed, Lady Mannering fed on it.

"See what you've done?" she said, self-satisfaction glowing in the voice. "Have you no idea what it would mean to all of us, especially the boys, to have a connection with Lord

Browning? It would erase in one stroke all the Mannering
scandals and your uncles' disgraceful . . ."

"Mama, stop at once," Colby pleaded. She could not permit
her mother to spew any more poison in the boys' hearing. "Go
back to Bath. I'll contrive a way to keep you there."

Hours after, when the house was quiet, Colby went to the
stables and saddled Midnight. Horse and rider moved like the
wind. The stallion caught her mood, and they flew over the
darkening land, a shadowy moonlight their only companion.

Her aunt's words about her mother's treatment of her father
ran around her brain, and the barren years spent in India came
back to her unbidden, years of watching her father sink into
silent resignation, while lesser men with more ambition and
guile achieved preferment over him.

Colby had known but never wanted to admit that her mother
was at the root of most of her father's failures. Phillida's
pushy ways, her scheming, her flirtations, her taunts and public humiliations were like a Greek chorus in the periphery of
the poor man's life. In time her father was moved from one
smaller and less socially correct outpost to another.

To make matters worse, Lady Mannering used what little
money there was to cut a pitiful swath in Calcutta and Delhi at
the height of the season and the hill country in summer, while
the family scrimped and did without to keep her as happy as
her sulfuric nature would allow.

Two years before, her uncles, having bled the estate white,
died within months of each other, and Aden Mannering inherited the title and the estate. Her mother was elated. She was
sure she had come into her own. At last she would be able to
live the life she saw as her due after years of blighted dreams
and aspirations. Only upon her return did she learn that she
was poor as a church mouse, shunned by her prosperous
neighbors, and worse, a figure of ridicule among the townspeople and the tenants. Her frustration knew no bounds. She
railed against a hostile fate, wearing her family down with her
discontent and sending her husband into his final decline.

Soon after her father died, Colby urged her mother to take
up the few invitations from old India friends who had retired

to Bath. Without a moment's hesitation or concern for Colby and the boys, Phillida departed in a cloud of cologne and mourning costumes her sister and daughter had hastily sewn, and there she remained until she had worn out her welcome. Not everyone, Colby was to learn, allowed themselves to be martyred by her difficult character.

Colby recalled her aunt telling her wistfully after one of Phillida's more violent attacks on Aden Mannering: "Father was a prosperous draper, but he always warned Phillida that she aimed too high."

The two had been sitting on the veranda of the commandant's house in one of the last of a series of shabby garrison towns.

"Papa liked Aden well enough to warn him that your mother and he wouldn't suit. But when has reason ever prevailed over a man in love with a beautiful, heart-shaped face and a frigid heart?"

Young as she was, Colby could not escape the feeling that her father had married the wrong woman, and while he might not have been aware of it, her aunt had never married because no man ever measured up to him. It had been a miserable tangle of twisted hopes and dreams that soured Colby early on love and marriage as nothing else could. And here I am now crying into the wind in a tangle of my own making. Was history to repeat itself?

Colby had let her mind pursue directions of its own, and when Midnight stumbled, she was brought back to the present more forcefully than she liked. She soothed the shaken horse and let him walk quietly in the light of the moon.

Twenty yards off in the darkness, Augustus Panaman raised himself in the saddle of his surefooted mountain pony, leveled a long hunting rifle, aimed, and let the hammer slam forward. No report followed.

Chapter 12

Nevil lay sprawled in an armchair next to the dying firelight in the library of Moreton, a half-empty decanter dangling from his hand, fitfully asleep. Suddenly he careened out of his chair. It took him a moment to identify the sound of pounding on the door. Cursing, he shook himself awake and carrying a large branch of candles, opened the door.

Colby, her eyes as untamed as her unbound hair, pushed past him and entered the library.

Nevil renewed the fire and waited for her to catch her breath. When he turned back, he was glad to see that Colby was as unsure as he was himself. He waited as she stood in the furthest reaches of the room, bracing himself for another assault on his ragged nerves by the look of her, still dressed in the breeches and the shirt he'd found her in that afternoon. He wavered between hope and despair, mad as hell that this strange woman held the key to his future.

Colby surveyed the room, her face ashen, her fingers never still. He waited for her to say something, and the moments lengthened long enough to drive him to distraction. To his surprise, Nevil heard himself say:

"You can have the loan you want."

He called himself every kind of fool for losing himself in her distress, but knew wild horses couldn't force him to take back his words. It wasn't what he wanted by a long shot, but he would live with it if he had to.

She whirled around, her shock equal to his. "I don't believe this."

"That's what you wanted," Nevil said, unwillingly moved

by the hollowness of her voice. He was unable to look at the hurt and pain in her eyes. He didn't like the changes that had come over her. Bold and commanding as she'd been in their other encounters, he had come to expect fire and ice. That Colby Mannering he could deal with.

"This smacks of charity," Colby said bitterly. Feeling suddenly cornered, she moved hurriedly to the middle of the room. More than anything, she wanted to accept it with thanks, but she knew herself too well. "I prefer our first bargain. It's a quid pro quo I can live with. I want nothing I have not earned, no matter how onerous that might be."

What she could not tell him was that his change of heart had come too late, much too late to save her. And for that she could thank her mother. In an odd way, she knew that for once she had to be grateful for her mother's self-centered, more pragmatic and honest view of the world. But she couldn't allow herself to cave in so easily. She straightened her spine. The old Colby was back and staring him down.

He took up the challenge. "We have gone beyond insulting each other. In truth, I must have an heir," Nevil said, trying to keep his voice in check, fearful of the tears that threatened. "My nephew and heir died last week."

At once Colby understood what she had only dimly suspected that afternoon. Where was the air of bred-in-the-bone certainty and high-handedness that Nevil had worn like a badge of honor in his scorn of her so loftily displayed in London? She had too many scars and too many sleepless nights to ever forgive him. Of course, she was sorry about his nephew's death, but she fought down the natural sympathy she might have felt for what she could plainly see was Browning's terrible loss.

"I need an answer, Lady Colby." Nevil wanted to be finished with her and the onerous mission that had sent him pounding down to the country.

Unwittingly, Browning's voice had regained the tone that had hurt Colby before. Demanding, impatient, it had the ring of a man who couldn't be bothered with niceties of feeling, except his own. She could have no idea how mistaken she was.

"Take the blasted loan or have my child on the terms you

offered in London, damn it, but let us come to an understanding."

Colby knew she was trapped. To take Browning's money
without earning it went against the core of her being. Independence and self-reliance had carried her through a difficult life
and were defenses she had learned to treasure.

She knew it would be years before she could even begin to
repay the loan. The debt would be a daily albatross, and she
knew herself well enough to know that she could not live with
that kind of obligation.

She had to ask herself again, did she have the right to deny
the boys all the intangible advantages of being related to one
of England's premiere families?

"I am waiting for your answer, Lady Colby." She was pro-
longing his agony when too many unsettled things awaited
him in London, not the least of which was tracking down
Robert's killer.

Colby knew there was no way out, knowing the answer she
gave now would determine the course of too many lives.

"I need time to think." She tried to keep her voice from giving away her inner storms.

"You have not been attending. I need to marry at once and
produce an heir." The last came out as close to a plea as
Browning could ever achieve. He hated the idea of it, and he
gritted his jaw and threw out at her all the pent-up horrors of
the last days. "Let us be frank. I have no interest in you other
than a brood mare, and you need my position to safeguard
your brothers. It is as good a bargain as you're ever likely to
receive, considering the reasons for your uncles' suicides."

Colby's head shot up and she stared dumbfounded. If he
was aware that her uncles had taken the easy way out of unmet
gambling debts, the most severe of all gentlemen's iniquities,
then all society must know. It went a long way toward explaining why the family was ostracized by everyone on their return
from India.

The trap closed irretrievably on Colby. All doubts, all un-
certainties were decided for her.

"Yes, my lord," she said in a strangled voice, seeking the
support of the nearest chair.

Nevil had used his trump card to advantage, but his victory was as hollow as Colby's surrender.

"That's settled then. I shall see that an announcement is placed in the *Times,* and we will be married at St. Margaret's, Westminster, in a sennight."

"So soon?"

"You are to be in London the day after tomorrow."

"The banns? You are in mourning."

"I am not hampered by the conventions," he said icily. "Money, Lady Colby, you will soon learn, smoothes everything, and there is a senile bishop in the family who will do the honors. If he refuses, there is always the special license."

Nevil walked to the door to escape seeing Colby's final surrender. He owed her that at least. But he underestimated his adversary once again.

Colby understood that the years ahead with this remote, obstinate man were going to be unadulterated purgatory unless she reasserted the terms of their hellish marriage, and she needed to get some of her own back quickly.

"Let us start the way we mean to go on," she said, keeping her voice hard. "I will not allow you to dictate to me in any way once I fulfill my part of this insanity. You live in London leading any life you desire, while I raise the child in the country. Is that clear?"

If Nevil needed any reminder that life with this woman would be one Cheltenham drama after the other, he had it now. He had thought they had settled everything, and here she was making conditions no gentlewoman would dare.

He returned to the center of the room barely able to control himself. For two pence he would scotch the whole thing and return to London unencumbered as he came.

Indeed, maybe he ought to settle for some well-bred, comfortable aristocratic beauty. He was on the point of telling Colby to take her soiled family and her viper's tongue out of his sight when the thought of such an alliance came full-grown into his mind. In his experience of them, their heads were full of cotton wool and moonlight. He shuddered visibly at having to dance attendance at Almack's and all the other institutions and rites of life he hated, but that were so necessary to a fashionable wife. The alternative to Colby died aborning. No woman he might choose would give him the breathing room he held so dear, and which she promised him. By the same token, he didn't want a virago dogging his heels, as Colby Mannering threatened to be.

"As soon as you are increasing, the less we see of each other the better," he said, not even trying to keep the edge out of his voice. "Does that suit you?"

"Perfectly," Colby replied, rising from the chair.

"Your sole responsibility until the wedding will be dancing attendance on my mother without ever letting her or anyone know the true circumstances. Can you do it?"

Colby nodded.

Nevil walked her to the door. "Understand this. You will have nothing to do with the wedding plans," he said. "Come directly to my house, and John Lear will see you settled and will arrange everything."

They left the room immediately, and he watched her settle herself into the saddle with the fluid grace that in any other woman would have elicited his admiration.

"Oh, yes. Nominate a male representative of the family to negotiate the marriage settlements," he added.

"I will conduct them," Colby said dully. "There is no one to act for me."

"Suit yourself," Nevil said, trying not to feel sorry for such a state of isolation as she described. He had achieved all he came to Moreton for and didn't want to say anything rash. He had already done that once, and he couldn't ask his guardian angel to extricate him once again.

As he turned to leave, Colby called out. "What do I call you?"

The question made him pause, almost as if an enormous obstacle had indeed arisen.

"Nevil will do. And I suppose I shall have to call you Colby. Silly name."

Colby threw him a look of sheer disgust, and was about to give Midnight the spur when she heard Browning call out from the top of the step.

"You've gained one victory. I've sacked Panaman," he called after her.

Colby said nothing and rode off, seething in the certain knowledge that she had sold her life to the highest bidder, and a bloody bastard at that. Still, life would be glorious for Mark and Matthew, her mother would have everything she had always wanted, and her aunt a comfortable old age. What more could she ask for?

The question hung in the air.

Chapter 13

On the outskirts of London, Nevil directed his horse toward Tarn Maitland's house in Manchester Square, trying to steer his mind away from Colby and the devil's own pact they had finally made between them.

Try as he could, he wasn't able to get out of his mind the way Colby had looked when he last saw her. Worn down by his calculated onslaught to bend her to his will, he was not at all happy with himself. The last straw, he suspected, was when he revealed what he and society knew about her uncles. People had long memories, and only his protection could bring convenient amnesia and restore the Mannering name.

Perhaps he should have made himself more agreeable, charitable, in fact, before she left his house, but he drew back at the idea. The last time he had given in to sentiment with a woman he had very nearly lost his soul. Some things didn't bear thinking about.

Nearing Hyde Park, Nevil focused on the search for Robert's slayer. If Tarn Maitland wasn't at home, he would leave a message. He must know the progress his men had made. A footman was at the door to take his horse and tell him the Captain and Lady Maitland were at home.

Nevil arrived to find them at tea with their children, noise and confusion everywhere. He wanted to retreat. His head ached, and his limbs hurt from the bruising ride to town. It was a scene he had never thought to see. Three small boys were climbing all over Maitland, who was pretending to be a mountain they could not scale. No quarter was given on either side, and the children squealed in delight as they flew in the air and landed on various couches and chairs. Who would credit that Captain Black and White, one of the most important men in London, would be seen this way?

Most of his friends who had children rarely saw them, and Nevil thought that was the way things should be. His own father didn't really acknowledge his existence until he was ten, and that was considered heretical. Yet here was a man who, if his eyes didn't misread the matter, was having the time of his life. Nevil could never imagine himself in Tarn's place, and Colby had assured him he had no worries on that head. He was more relieved than he could say.

"Dear Nevil, let me spare you this unseemly circus." Lady Barbara came to his rescue. A distant relative, he only began to know her when she married Maitland six years before. She was the kindest and most understanding of women, and he was grateful for her intervention. She and Tarn were the happiest of married couples, and she would know why he had come to see them. With the help of an old nanny and nursery maid, she led the children away.

"You will want to know what we have learned," Maitland said, pouring drinks for them when quiet returned.

"Yes."

"It was almost too easy," Maitland said, his face somber. "The killer was a common footpad, and his friends nothing better. The Bow Street runners have him in charge, and he will swing for Robert's murder."

"He wasn't put up to it? Robert's friends were barely scratched."

"I was sure you would want to know that. My men looked into that rather vigorously," Maitland said ruefully. "No connection has been found between that band of cutthroats and Jeffrey Coon, if that's what you're asking."

"You are absolutely certain, Tarn?"

"Jeffrey was in London, sprawled drunk over a card table at Boodles, and the villains say they don't know him from Adam."

Nevil walked around the room, idly picking up bric-a-brac and returning them unseen, trying to calm himself.

"I'm glad of that," he said softly at last. "I would have killed him with my bare hands."

"I knew that. My men don't leave loose ends," Tarn observed proudly.

"Thank you." He fell into the nearest chair. He couldn't trust his legs.

Lady Barbara returned to the room and stood by her husband's side.

"What are your plans now, Nevil?" Barbara asked.

"Why do you ask?" Surely they could not know about Colby Mannering.

"We have asked Lady Miriam to spend some time at Maitland House, to recuperate and to get away from all reminders of Robert for a spell," Lady Barbara said, getting her husband's approval first.

"I think that's a wonderful idea," Nevil replied, still not certain that was the reason for the collusion. "What else have you to tell me?"

"Will you go to Paris for the Foreign Office?" Maitland asked, lighting one of his famous cheroots, the size of a cudgel. "We have news that there is grave unrest among the Bonapartists. It is not in England's interests to have political upheaval in France at present."

"I couldn't turn my mind off Robert so quickly," Nevil argued.

"It is exactly what you need," Maitland insisted. "You are well known and admired in Paris and exactly what we need."

One of the best-kept secrets in all of London was Nevil's occasional secret assignments undertaken on behalf of the Foreign Office, a job that Maitland had secured for him. Even now Nevil could remember every word Tarn Maitland had used to recruit him.

"You are too good a man to waste your life as just another rich London wastrel," Tarn had roared at him one night after a notorious revel with his friends. They had staged a drunken medieval joust in the park, with Nevil and another man in ancient suits of armor atop a lurching coach.

"There'll be no medals or glory for you, but it will give your life some purpose other than scapegrace outrages," Maitland had said.

For Nevil it had been a turning point in a life warped by his years of battle in the Peninsula. And for that Browning would follow Captain Black and White into hell.

Nevil became aware that the Maitlands waited for his answer.

"There's one small obstacle. I am to be married soon," Nevil said.

The Maitlands were overjoyed, and the room rang with their happiness for him. Everything in Nevil rose up to protest the travesty he was planning, but he could not spoil their joy or admit his own unease.

"Perfect," Maitland said at last. "Take your wedding trip to Paris. What could be more natural?"

"Of course," Lady Maitland seconded. "But tell us, who is the girl, and why have you kept her from us?"

Nevil said as little as he could, afraid that he would succumb to Barbara's penetrating intelligence and admit the truth. He escaped soon after on the pretext that he had to tell his mother his news.

Chapter 14

John Lear paid off the cab that brought Colby from the inn where the London coach had deposited her.

Colby's mood was in no way different from her earlier arrival at Browning's house. If possible, it was, in fact, worse. She was feeling lost and confused by the swift change of events. She had even less money in her reticule, and it cost her much to ask the cabman to wait while she found someone within to pay her fare.

The thought of being Lady Colby Browning in a few days' time, with money to burn for every luxury she could want, did not lighten the moment one whit. If anything, it made her feel on a level with any woman of the evening who accepted money for services performed. She had, in fact, a good deal more regard for a common prostitute than she had for herself. Her mind reeled with disgust.

If she needed any reminder of the dubious alteration in her status since she had last seen the young secretary, his attitude toward her said it all. Cold and formal, Lear seated Colby in the drawing room and stood over her with none of the warmth he had shown on the long walk back to her hotel two weeks ago. Then he had been all concern and consideration for his employer's poor treatment of her.

Colby was not at all wrong in her estimate. From a loan, Lear told himself, the Lady Colby had promoted herself into a marriage, which he sensed from his observations was becoming a torment to both parties. She was anything but a gushing bride-to-be. It hadn't taken him long to guess the terms of the forthcoming nuptials. Always a romantic, John Lear wasn't sure whether his distaste was more for Colby or for Nevil. He expected nobility of his betters and was bitterly disappointed when they acted any less.

"I have booked three communicating suites for you at Farran's," he announced in a chilling voice. "You will need a maid, but I have engaged our underbutler to see to your other needs." Lear extracted a large envelope bulging with money, which he handed to her as if it soiled his fingers.

"Thank you," Colby said, her tone matching his. Two could play at outraged morality, she decided. "I should like to retire there at once."

If I am to be the wife of a paragon, I might as well start now by being unfeeling toward others. But the very idea revolted her as soon as she realized what she was doing. *What's happening to me? I, of all people, abominate the Quality when they treat their minions like so much furniture.* Colby rose wearily to her feet, hating the changes that were taking place in her.

Suddenly Lear realized that his unreasoning prejudice against Colby for marrying Nevil for his money had blinded him until that moment to the distress she was now suffering. She appeared more miserable than when Browning first sent her away. The spirit and courage that had first drawn his admiration were gone. He saw that her marvelous eyes were ringed with lines of fatigue, her hands shook as she held the envelope. *Who am I,* he asked himself, *innocent in the ways of the ton, to judge anyone's motives for marrying well?*

"May I have the privilege of escorting you to the hotel?" he asked, reanimating warmly toward her.

Colby was instantly alert to Lear's turnabout, even if she did not understand its origins. It cheered Colby enormously and brought tears to her eyes. She nodded, and they proceeded to leave the house, where a carriage waited at the curb.

"Lord Nevil has put this coach at your disposal," Lear said, handing her into the gleaming black vehicle. He seated her with every ceremony and took his place across the way.

"After you have rested, I have been instructed to take you to a dressmaker, who will prepare a wardrobe for you, especially a costume for your meeting tomorrow morning with his lord-ship's mother."

Colby stared at Lear. The idea of meeting her future mother-in-law threw her into a tailspin. In her single-minded quest, she had never given thought to all the ramifications of her marriage to Browning and cursed her failure to anticipate this of all meetings.

"Must I meet Lady Browning so soon?" she heard herself blurt out and tried to recover the lapse. Colby had spoken her alarums aloud and could have bitten her tongue. The whole world didn't have to know the truth of her state, nor the poverty of her wardrobe. She fell into a miserable silence, hoping she hadn't actually given away too much.

"I lost a bet with myself," Lear said, trying to break the un-comfortable impasse. "I thought you would wonder how the dressmaker would know your size."

"And how does she?"

Lear blushed. "I gave her a fair idea of your . . . dimensions, your ladyship."

Colby laughed, and the two finished the drive to the hotel in their former charity with each other.

Chapter 15

Nevil Browning arrived at the hotel the next morning moments after Colby finished her toilette.

Despite a sleepless night, she looked better than she felt, and that, Colby considered, had more to do with the London dressmaker's arts than anything she had contributed. Unused to such finery, nor with any uncommon interest in the way she looked, Colby couldn't help being happy with the way the green velvet dress molded provocatively over her full breasts and narrow hips. She admired the way the overskirt moved magically with each step she took before the huge three-sided mirror. If I don't watch myself, I shall become a fashion plate like Mama, and she cringed at the thought.

The butler announced Nevil's arrival, and Colby went reluctantly into the overly ornate drawing room. Nevil was standing at the long windows studying people in the park beyond when Colby entered. Dressed in a severe black coat with narrow black trousers over gleaming black boots, he was shifting a tall hat draped for mourning from one hand to the other. His shoulders, normally straight and arrogant, bespeaking his days as a regimental officer, were slumped, Colby noted. He stood in an attitude that in any other man at any other time would have touched Colby's heart.

He turned and acknowledged her presence with a formal bow.

"Before we leave, I would like you to wear this." He took a small jeweler's box from an inside pocket. "I should like my mother to think I gave you this sometime ago. It is the ring all Browning women wear during their betrothal."

Colby took the box and opened it. The ring was old, a cir-
clet of diamonds and emeralds. It was the most beautiful ring
she had ever seen, and she yearned to try it on, but couldn't
allow herself to wear it.

"I would be dishonoring all the women who have worn this
before."

"Lady Colby, don't try me," Nevil said, exasperated.
Wouldn't this woman ever do anything without an argument!

"My mother is waiting for us, and she would suspect there
was something wrong with the betrothal."

With painful, shaking fingers Colby slipped the ring on.

"I shall return it after the wedding," Colby said quietly and
turned to leave the room.

Nevil stopped her.

"It is difficult for me, but I must ask you one more favor,"
Browning said, turning red with each word. "I have led her to
believe that this is a love match."

For the first time Colby looked at him directly, speechless at
the pain she saw. He is human after all, but the thought gave
her little consolation.

"You see, I had to give her some hope after Robert's death,"
he said, dropping his eyes and rolling his hat between his fingers.

She nodded and followed him out of the suite. With every
word between them, Colby was struck by the enormity of what
she had gotten herself into. She blamed her uncles, who had
forced these lies and evasions on her. I've mortgaged my life,
and I can't do anything about it.

The drive to Lady Miriam's was accomplished too quickly
for Colby's nerves. Sitting alone with her future husband in a
close carriage, both sunk in a gloom they could not escape,
was for Colby a precursor of their life together.

She did not mean to subject herself to many such occasions
once she was safely increasing. At once Colby went cold and
hot by turns. Beads of perspiration started between her breasts
and a sensation of weakness she had never known made her
legs turn to jelly. She took a lawn handkerchief from her
sleeve and dried her hands.

On his side of the carriage, Nevil was covertly watching,

struck suddenly by her regal air, stately figure, and yes—he had to admit—her lovely face. Indeed, he thought, she will do as a long-distance wife and mother.

Hidden behind the curtains of her drawing room, it took all of Lady Miriam's considerable will to keep from rushing to the front hall to greet her new daughter. In appearance, at least, the unsmiling girl alighting from the carriage was all she could have wanted in wife for Nevil.

When at last her magisterial butler announced their arrival, Lady Miriam threw all restraint to the winds and folded Colby in her arms.

"Forgive my want of address, my dear," Lady Miriam said, releasing Colby at last, "but I have dreamed of the moment my son would present me with a wife for too long to hide my feelings as I should."

At once Nevil's fears underwent a sea change. The two women drifted to a sofa, holding hands and chattering as if they'd known each other an age. In his dealings with Colby, he had only seen iron austerity. Suddenly she was smiling and relaxed, a different woman. If Colby was acting a part, she was doing it well, and he was able to breathe easily for the first time in weeks.

Like most, Colby had fallen under his mother's powerful personality. He'd done the right thing. Lady Miriam was clearly recovering from her terrible grief far more quickly than he'd ever imagined. and the cold knot that had surrounded his heart since Robert's death began to thaw a little.

Nevil had been dreading the first encounter between these two strong women, afraid that they would dislike each other on sight, and he was inordinately pleased to have worried for naught.

"I must hear about this secret betrothal of yours," Lady Browning announced merrily.

Colby and Nevil exchanged agonizing glances.

"What has Nevil told you?" Colby asked with great presence of mind. "I would not want to repeat anything."

"I told Mother, my love," Nevil said, almost tripping over

the endearment that came so hard, "that you would love to tell her all the details."

"You are as bad as your father was," Lady Miriam laughed. "He hated seeming to be romantic, but he was all the same."

"Oh, yes, he is very romantic." If Nevil wanted her to act the fond fiancée, he would have to take the consequences.

Colby's fertile imagination spun out scenes of courtship and surrender among the bucolic wonders of Brawleigh and Moreton. She was hard-pressed to think of persuasive words and pictures to warm the older woman's heart, but her immediate affection for the unstinted warmth she had received added genius to the recital.

"Really, Nevil, dear, you must help me remember some of our amorous moments," Colby said. Why should I shoulder all this lying?

"You're doing splendidly, my darling," he said, beginning to enjoy the game she had started.

"Indeed, he's trying, Lady Miriam," Colby replied in what she hoped were properly gushing tones. "Men seem only interested in the chase. As soon as I succumbed to his tearful protestations of undying love and devotion, he began to take me for granted."

Lady Miriam listened to the exchange with a mounting dismay that she did not want them to see. She couldn't put her finger on the discordant note she felt between Nevil and Colby, and didn't mean to try, for the moment at least. But she knew her son too well to accept the timing of this too convenient love match. It was too pat and too soon after Robert's death to sit well with her.

Miriam Browning knew herself to be a shrewd observer of people, and her quick acceptance of Colby Mannering was neither whim nor sham. Within moments she succumbed to the girl's great natural dignity. Colby carried herself as a lady should. Behind those extraordinary eyes she sensed reserves of what she preferred to think were character and intelligence. And best of all, Colby had none of the practiced, cloying ways of most of the young girls she met each Season, and that spoke volumes to her.

Lady Browning knew little about recent Mannering history,

except rumors of ungentlemanly irregularities, but she remembered Aden Mannering as an Adonis in a smart army officer uniform and knew her husband had been exceedingly fond of him. And that was recommendation enough.

Listening to the moonshine about their courtship—for she suspected that was what she had been hearing—she was unable to credit her son as a rural Lothario. But what mother could imagine what her son would be like in the throes of rioting passion? Nevil was about to be married to a wildly attractive and thoroughly acceptable woman, and that was sufficient to be going on with. And if Colby meant to lead her son a merry chase, so much the better. Hadn't she done it to Nevil's father, with the result they never had a boring moment in a long and happy marriage?

She felt suddenly sanguine about the future. Her grief for her beloved grandson lifted a little. Life would go on. One door closes and another opens, she told herself, and sighed audibly.

"Lady Miriam, we are tiring you," Colby said, rising to her feet. She and Nevil had been keeping up a false line of chatter that died at once when they realized that she was no longer attending.

"I am not at all, my dear, but I am sure you must have many things to attend to for the wedding," Lady Miriam said. "I shall arrange a few small dinners."

"But you are in mourning," Colby protested. The thought that she would have to keep up the role of innocent infatuation before strangers was more than she could bear. She had counted on the family's bereavement to save her from the usual rounds of parties on the eve of the ceremony.

Lady Miriam saw the girl's panic, even if she did not completely understand it, and hastened to reassure her.

"I shall keep the company within the family," Lady Miriam assured her, and led them to the door.

Their return to the hotel was accomplished in hostile discomfort. Nevil watched Colby play idly with the ring on her finger, and for the first time he noticed that she wore no other jewelry or ornaments. How strange she was. Several times he thought to start a conversation, but the forbidding look on her face stopped him.

"I don't like lying, and I rely on you to keep occasions when I must do so to a minimum," Colby said when they came within sight of the hotel.

"I have no more wish than you do, but I ask you to be forbearing a little longer."

"But I am not a patient woman. You should know that from the start."

"Oh, I do," he laughed, but he had precious little time to enjoy it.

"I intend to finish the settlements this day."

"John Lear and Mr. Cortnage, my man of business, are at your disposal." Would she never be at ease with him or herself?

"I want you there," she said coldly. "As I said before, do your own dirty work."

"You charmed my mother, and for that I thank you," he said, seeking to be civil. Every time I try to be reasonable with this woman, Nevil told himself bitterly, she turns it into a battle royal. He was unaccustomed to difficult women, and he didn't like his first experience of it. It was fatiguing, and his head began to throb.

"Your mother made my task easy," she conceded in a gentle voice. "But I cannot promise I can continue to delude her. She doesn't deserve lies."

Nevil couldn't have agreed with her more.

"I admire her very much, and I will never do anything to earn her dislike, but I can't promise a return performance of rampant young love."

"Nor can I," he laughed again. "But I shall try to shield you from a repetition of today."

"See that you do."

Nevil threw up his hands.

Chapter 16

The atmosphere around the table in Colby's suite was thick with smoke and suppressed fury. She had taken on Lear, Cortnage, and Nevil in a hard round of bargaining over the settlements.

"With respect, Lady Mannering," the little man of business protested, "you cannot hope to manage two estates at once. You need a man . . ."

"Can I not?" she said, cutting him off without ceremony. With each moment he came to look like an evil toad. "I will not be done out of the money and other advantages Panaman was given for managing Moreton."

Cortnage appealed to Nevil, but he had long retired from the fray.

"Give Lady Colby everything she asks, and let us be done with this." The haggling over terms had long since soured Nevil, and he wanted to be away. He picked up his hat and left without another word.

After agreeing on the few outstanding issues, Cortnage assembled his papers and departed. Panaman had not exaggerated, Lady Colby was an unseemly bitch. She would make his life intolerable, and he dreaded the future.

Lear stayed on. His admiration for the way Colby had bested them knew no bounds. "I have seldom seen Cortnage so upset. You are a wonder."

"I am marrying for money, but I shall give good value."

"I have no doubt of it," he assured her. Once again she had amazed him. She had guessed his earlier disappointment in her reason for marrying Nevil Browning, but it wasn't as cold-blooded as he had first believed. John almost felt sorry for Browning. She would not be a comfortable wife.

Chapter 17

Cortnage, dusty and worn down by his hurried trip from London, stood in the middle of the cave, anxiously surveying the arsenal and food Augustus Panaman had stored in a corner.

Far from the well-barbered, proud peacock of his days as Browning's feared estate manager, Panaman looked like a fevered, fanatic hermit. He had grown a straggly beard, his hair was long and matted, and his eyes glinted with hate. Cortnage was alarmed at the change in the man, but he had other concerns to worry him.

"Lady Colby is a she-devil," Cortnage complained.

"Aye, afraid you'll not get the money I been sharing with you?" Panaman cackled. "Mind she doesn't look into all your fiddles. Browning won't like knowing about the fortune you made off him these many years."

Panaman wasn't saying anything the man of business hadn't been telling himself on the long ride down from London.

"That's why I'm here," he said, biting his lips.

"Want me to get rid of her, do you?"

"Remember, it was your idea in the first place," Cortnage said, trying to distance himself from the act.

"When I kill her, it will be for the way she's ruined my life, not to accommodate you," Panaman said, picking up a lethal-looking hunting rifle, caressing it like he would a woman. "She humiliated me, and she'll pay for it."

"And how will you do that if she's in London?" Cortnage asked.

"She loves Brawleigh and those two brats," the other replied shrewdly. "I can wait."

Chapter 18

The London Colby traversed, with bulging flimsies in her reticule, was far different from the one that had greeted her only a month before. Then her pockets had been almost empty and she had been too preoccupied with the bankruptcy that threatened Brawleigh to enjoy herself. The crowds of people at every turn, the noise of twopenny newspaper boys and food hawkers, and horses and carriages clogging the public roads were treats she hadn't the ease of mind to appreciate earlier.

Unlike Calcutta, which she knew from the family's years in India, London was relatively clean and free of importuning beggars, tragic crippleds, and snake charmers, freaks, and roaming cattle. If the air of London was not as sweet or as quiet as the country, there were other things to delight the senses, not the least of which were the elegant houses and numerous shops fitted out like treasure troves.

Colby smiled down at Ilene Merl, the clever, robust maid recommended by Barbara Maitland. The girl proudly carried the purchases her mistress had made. Among them were watches for her brothers, a smart hat and matching pelisse for her aunt, and a ring for her mother. Books on the latest farming methods and management were all Colby desired for herself.

But her first and most satisfying stop had been to Avery Meredith's bookshop, where she repaid him the money he had given her on account and she retrieved the books she had left with him. She bought some books for the family, and he wished her well on her marriage.

"My lady, you must not forget your appointments with the hairdresser and dressmaker at the hotel," the maid cautioned as Colby idled along Bond Street later in the morning.

The thought of the hours she must stand to be fitted for her wedding clothes and a trousseau befitting Nevil Browning's wife were a torment. Having her long, black hair trimmed and curled in the current mode was an additional trial, but she comforted herself with the knowledge that all this would soon be at an end. After the wedding and a brief honeymoon she would return to Brawleigh and, freed of all social and marital obligations, would do as she damn well pleased.

Colby, feeling more the thing, returned to the hotel with her abigail.

Hours later Colby waited for Nevil and another of the dismal parties he and his mother had arranged to introduce her to a select number of distant family members and close friends. She hated being on view, weighed up and measured like a prize sow.

Years of hosting parties for army officers and their wives and a succession of chinless, officious pukka sahibs who worked for John, the name people like to use when speaking of the East India Company, had taught her how to smile and chat about the most inconsequential subjects as if each word were a piece of wisdom for the ages. The skill stood her well.

"My dear Lady Colby, you are a wonder," Barbara Maitland had whispered to her at Lady Miriam's house the night before. "It must be torture for you, but you seem to be taking it in stride. I congratulate you."

Colby smiled and took Lady Barbara's hand.

"Society is most anxious to see the lady who has captured Nevil's heart," Barbara laughed.

A woman of great warmth and perspicacity, she had not missed the occasional scowl and strain she had seen cross Colby's face. It confirmed what Lady Barbara and her husband has suspected. Nevil and Colby were entering into a marriage of convenience, and her heart bled for them. Her own engagement had started off badly, but luck and a kinder fate intervened to make the Maitlands the marriage ideal.

"London was most curious about me, too," Lady Barbara explained. "What was their legendary Captain Black and White thinking of when he wed a penniless cripple?" For emphasis, Lady Barbara waved the handsome cane she sometimes carried.

"Barbara, don't crown my bride-to-be so soon," Nevil said, coming up to them, pretending a lightheartedness he was far from feeling. He had been watching the tête-à-tête nervously, afraid that Barbara, with her sharp understanding, would learn the truth.

He kissed Colby on the cheek for all to see, and slipped his arm through hers. "Don't tell my fiancée my many failings."

"You needn't fear, my lord," Colby said sharply, disengaging her arm. "Your horrid reputation is well preserved."

"And will you restore it?" Lady Barbara asked, hoping for clues to her suspicions.

"I am not a reformer and have no taste for the impossible," Colby said, leaving them abruptly to speak to other guests, but not before she saw Nevil's embarrassment and Barbara's consternation.

Colby was not proud of her performance and in her review of the night before didn't hear Nevil enter the suite. When she turned around, she was stunned to see him wearing the full dress uniform of a captain in the Light Horse, a clutch of ribbons and medals on his tight, red-and-gold tunic. A tall, flaring shako with the bugle insignia shining from it was under his arm, and a ceremonial sword rested along the skin-tight, blue-gray trousers.

"I didn't know you had been in the Peninsula," she said, unable to hide her amazement.

"There is a lot you don't know about me," he said curtly. Obviously, he was still smarting from her setdown before Barbara Maitland.

"Were you with Wellington?"

"Of course."

"Where?"

"Many places, but Badajoz was the last," he said tightly.

With her father as her instructor, Colby knew the history of every major battle of the war in the Peninsula. Badajoz was one of the fiercest battles ever encountered by the British Army.

In spite of herself, Colby was impressed. Her father had received many letters from old army comrades describing the bloody fighting. She knew that the price for possession of the key fortress of Western Spain, without which Wellington could not rout Napoleon, was five thousand British and Portuguese casualties, thirty-five hundred of them the flower of the British Army.

Riding together to the first of two parties that night, the air was more charged than usual. At the best of times neither had the inclination or talent for meaningless talk.

"Lady Colby, I desire you to keep a rein on your tongue tonight," Nevil said, breaking the leaden silence as the carriage turned into Manchester Square. "I did not appreciate your comments to Lady Barbara about my reputation. After dinner I will escort you to my regimental ball, and I expect you to remember the world need not know of your disillusionment."

"I'm not dressed . . ." she started to say.

"And I am supposed to be in mourning. But we are going because I have never missed my regiment's great occasions," he said in a tight voice. "My mother insisted we attend so that you may be seen by more Londoners."

Colby was at once contrite. She knew she had been unforgivably rude when she had engaged to play the hoyden in front of Barbara Maitland. It was proving to be a pyrrhic victory. The sight of him in his uniform, the knowledge that he had somehow survived unscathed at Badajoz shifted something inside her. She did not want to think what it was.

"You needn't worry," Colby said coolly, masking her real feelings.

The Maitlands were famous for their hospitality, and the dinner party went off without incident. Colby behaved civilly, pretending an interest in every word Nevil uttered in her hearing.

"My dear Colby, how wonderful. I hear you are to travel to Paris," Lady Miriam said as they waited for their carriages at the end of the evening.

"Mama, I told you it was a secret," Nevil quickly put in when he saw Colby's head snap up in dismay.

"How romantic," Barbara chimed in, trying to defuse matters and give Colby time to recover. "Remember to buy your bride all the clothes and jewelry she covets."

"Of course." Nevil threw Lady Barbara a grateful smile and quickly steered Colby through the door.

"What is this about Paris?" Colby stormed as the carriage door closed on them.

"We have to go somewhere. People expect it," he said lamely. "Most women would be overjoyed."

"I am not most women, and I thought I made that perfectly clear to you from the beginning."

Nevil laughed in agreement. To be sure, he knew few women who could hold a candle to Colby Mannering's sulfuric temper. That made him look at her almost as if it were the first time. He really saw the wickedly defiant eyes, the perfect, smooth skin, her wonderful, rounded bosom heaving. They were a handful, and his lips twitched, his fingers kneading. To his intense discomfort, the idea of taming them and her was almost irresistible. The heat that rose in him was an unwelcome sign that Colby was reaching him in ways he hadn't planned or considered possible.

"I will not go to Paris," he heard Colby say. "I cannot afford the time away from Brawleigh and Moreton House."

"You will go because I have to go, and that's final," he said.

Colby reared up as if struck. The tone was too much. "I will not be spoken to in that way."

"Let's understand each other," he said between gritted teeth. "I'll speak to you any way I like."

"You promised to get out of my life once I was . . ." and the words, too delicate to mention, died in her throat.

"I mean to, but I need you with me in Paris," he said.

"Why?"

"You need not know," he said, happy they had arrived at the ball.

"I'm not moving until you tell me."

Too unused to explaining his actions to anyone, no matter how high-handed, Nevil lost his temper.

"Leave off. It is not healthy for you to know." He took her arm roughly as they descended the carriage steps.

Colby was an instant success. Guests were streaming toward the garden when she and Nevil arrived. They were immediately surrounded and bathed in congratulations on their wedding the next day.

The officers could not get their fill of the tall, willowy woman in the lavender silk dress, cut low to display deep cleavage and clinging to accentuate her long, slim legs. The women stood transfixed, unable to hide their admiration for Nevil, who stood at her side, magnetic in his uniform, aware that few of his brother officers could match him.

The master of ceremonies called the gathering to order and reminded them that the tattoo was about to begin. The throng moved through stately windows which led out to where the regimental band in all its finery was massed on a wide, rolling lawn lit by massive flambeaux. It was a clear, chilly evening, but few minded. The full and colorful pageantry of a storied regiment was a familiar ritual to Colby, but it never failed to stir her profoundly.

With the drill unfolding and the rousing, marching music floating on the slight breeze, Colby looked over at Nevil, expecting to see him blasé and unaffected by the sight. He was standing at attention, a look of pain on his face enough to touch a heart of stone. For the second time that evening, the man she had written off as cold and devoid of feeling showed a side she didn't expect.

For Nevil, hearing the band play "St. Patrick's Day" and other martial airs, his friends in their smart uniforms that had never seen battle, all the panoply of the peacetime army so vastly different from war, drove his mind back unwillingly to Badajoz for the second time that night. With it came the memories and nightmares he had spent eight years trying to keep at bay with drink and devilry.

Nine o'clock, April 6, 1812, and the events that followed were etched in his memory like a stone marker. He saw again the men assigned to make the first assault on the fortress when they were discovered shortly before zero hour by the light of a burning carcass thrown from the rampart. He relived the sight of long lines of red uniforms marching forward like streams of burning lava in the crash of hundreds of shells and powder barrels thrown at them, blowing them to bits in a fireball that turned night into day.

Once again his own last memories of his leg giving way . . . falling into a ditch full of a writhing mass of dead and wounded like himself. All were trampled by comrades in a rush to avenge the fallen and reach the breaches and win the town, the day, the battle. And then there was the darkness, the mercy of unconsciousness. But wounds of the flesh and the mind were a battle he had never won.

Colby couldn't take her eyes off Nevil, grim and closed away from those who surrounded him. An instinct she didn't want to question made her edge closer to him.

"You seemed far away," she said in a soft voice when he turned toward her a little while later.

"I was."

She saw him shudder and felt inexplicably drawn to him. She reached out to touch his arm, but he turned away, shutting her out as completely as the closing of a door.

Chapter 19

"Really, Colby, you might have chosen a more elegant wedding dress than this," Lady Mannering sniffed, circling her daughter. "You have all the money in Christendom, my girl. Flaunt it."

"Leave her be. She looks a treat," Sylvia Rainwriter cut in, admiring her niece in the simple, flowing satin dress devoid of all decoration. "Left to you she'd look like a Christmas tree."

Colby stood apart from the wrangling. Her mind continued to dwell on Nevil's anguish of the night before. On the way home from the ball, she had tried to draw him out.

"I am not in the habit of explaining myself," he had said shortly. "I do not trust personal confidences between men and women."

Considerably chastened, Colby retreated to her corner of the carriage, and the rest of the journey was made in bitter silence.

But now, as she waited for her maid to complete her coiffure and Lear to escort them to the church, she couldn't still her curiosity. She wasn't sure she liked knowing that Nevil Browning was not exactly the one-dimensional man she'd reluctantly agreed to marry. It suggested depths she had not anticipated and a humanity that might not be easy to ignore in her future dealings with him.

Colby was soon distracted with the arrival of John Lear. He had driven to Brawleigh to escort the family to London the day before and was on the best terms with her brothers and aunt. Her mother had ignored him, Aunt Sylvia had told Colby, as if he were beneath her touch.

"As soon as Mr. Lear said he was the son of the vicar who

had the living in a Browning estate in Cornwall, your mother dismissed him," Miss Rainwriter explained. "Phillida has always been a snob, but your marriage to Lord Nevil is sending her into the stratosphere. You must talk with her."

Colby intended to, but for the moment she had other things to occupy her, chief of which was the jeweler's box Lear was handing her. She opened it, and her breath caught in her throat. A tiara and choker of huge, flawless diamonds sparkled like stars in a moonless sky.

"His lordship asks that you wear these today," Lear said, awkward with the errand he'd been given. "They are the Browning diamonds, and customarily worn on such occasions."

"I won't have them, John," Colby replied, closing the box defiantly and handing them back to him.

"You have to, Colby."

Miss Rainwriter, the only other witness to the scene, could only guess at Colby's refusal of the jewels. They had forgotten her presence.

"Colby, I wish to see you in the next room," the older lady said in a commanding voice that startled her niece.

"What is going on between you and that young man and the matter of the jewelry?" Miss Rainwriter asked, all normal, demure behavior disappearing.

"John Lear is the only friend I have in London who understands my reasons for marrying Browning," Colby said, glad to admit the truth.

"You still have not formed even the smallest affection for Nevil?" she asked, incredulous.

"I loathe him, and he loathes me," Colby said.

"No, Colby," Miss Rainwriter cried. "You cannot marry him if you feel that. I won't let you sacrifice yourself."

"Can't I?" Colby broke down, slipping into a chair, burying her face in her arms.

Her aunt dropped to the carpet and leaned down beside her. "I suspected this from the beginning."

Colby heard her and stood. "I'm sorry; that was wrong of me. And I was wrong about the jewelry, too."

Her aunt watched Colby stand and brace her shoulders and dry her eyes. "Come, we will be late."

Taking Sylvia's arm, they reentered the drawing room.

"John, help me with the jewelry."

The slanting rain that pounded London that morning broke long enough for John Lear to escort Colby to the church door. Captain Maitland, who had offered to stand locum parentis for Colby, walked her gravely down the aisle of the church, where a handful of guests waited in the front pews.

Too weighed down by the enormity of what lay ahead, Colby kept her gaze averted, unaware that Nevil looked at her with new eyes. The severe elegance of her dress, the winsome figure she made, appearing to float on Maitland's arm, was more disturbing than he wanted to admit.

Only moments before Colby entered, Nevil had been thinking about Gracia Alvarez, the dark-haired, dark-eyed, fiery Portuguese beauty he'd been engaged to months before Badajoz. He had loved her with a full and melting heart until the day he returned from a succession of army hospitals. While his wounds had healed, he came back to her gaunt and gray, his body and mind scarred with the pain and horrors he'd lived through. Gracia had recoiled at his touch. Once she had welcomed him, indeed, had thrown herself into his arms and his bed when he was whole, a surpassingly handsome British deliverer. Their young, raging passion for each other overcame her convent breeding and his sense of honor. That was another time, another world, he reminded himself.

Dragged back to the present and the sight of Colby, ethereal and lovelier than he had seen her, drove all the bitter memories of Gracia from his mind. A feeling of hopefulness so long absent from his life, so unexpected, made him look at his bride in a new light.

Tarn Maitland delivered Colby to the altar and took his place as best man beside Nevil. With the rites quickly over, Nevil lifted Colby's veil and kissed her. It was a chaste kiss, but Colby drew back, shaken by the full and not unpleasant pressure of his lips.

The breakfast party with its endless toasts strained Colby's endurance. She yearned for a place to rest and some relief from the throbbing that threatened to split her head.

"My dear, dear daughter," Lady Miriam said as Colby and Nevil tried to make a silent exit. "I dreamed this moment for years, and you are all I wanted for Nevil."

She kissed her new daughter warmly.

"You are a godsend, and I know Robert would have approved," the old lady said softly.

Colby was moved to tears, feeling more like a lying interloper than ever. She wanted to tell Lady Miriam the truth, but knew it would be wrong. All Colby could hope was that a grandchild would fulfill the old lady's hopes, and the thought brought a becoming flush to her face. To cover her confusion, Colby pressed Lady Miriam's hands and kissed the wrinkled cheek.

Lady Miriam was not deceived. The evidence of her own eyes over the past days was enough to tell her how things went with her son and his bride. She had imparted her doubts to Lady Barbara, who had stood as daughter to her since coming to London as Captain Black and White's wife. The soul of discretion, Barbara would neither confirm nor deny the unsettling state of the marriage.

Chapter 20

Nevil's yacht rolled and pitched in the high seas that buffeted them across the Channel.

Below deck, Colby retched, her stomach churning, the luxurious fittings in the main cabin creaking in their holdings. A brass chandelier swayed like an inverted metronome overhead each time she opened her eyes.

"Master says you will feel better if you eat something," Ilene said, barely able to control her own seasickness, the tray she carried listing dangerously over the bed.

"Tell him to go to hell, and you with him," Colby managed to say, leaning over the covers trying to find the basin she'd ordered placed there.

The maid withdrew and went up on deck with her tray.

Nevil was enjoying himself hugely. Beside him the captain of the ship was in much the same condition as she'd left her mistress.

"Off to your bed, Captain Davids," she heard him say. "Leave your post to the first mate. He and I will manage."

Nevil turned from the rail and saw her green and pinched face.

"Go below. I'll see to Lady Colby." He took the tray and followed her down.

Colby heard the door open and Nevil's laugh at the sight of her. She hated to be seen so defenseless, her hair coming undone with the first wave of seasickness. She knew she must smell like a nursery basin.

"Get out," Colby whimpered, expecting him to leave in disgust, as any gentleman would.

"The waters are glorious," he said playfully. "Come on deck. The cold air will make you feel better."

Colby hadn't much strength, but she managed to sail a pillow at his head. He caught it and came to the bed.

"What you need is champagne and bananas," he said, trying to keep his eyes from her long, perfect legs spread across the bed, her skirts riding high on her body. He tried to imagine what it would be like to run his hands inside those enticing legs as far as they would go, his lips following the path they would take. His breath caught in his throat. He willed his blood to cool.

The thought of making love to Colby had come to him at the oddest moments in the last few days. What a turnup. He knew he was a fool to expect that anything more than the coldest act of procreation, achieved as quickly as possible, was all Colby would tolerate. The kind of abandon he had shared with Gracia was out of the question. And that was fine with him. He'd long since forsworn losing his heart to any woman again, much less one as unyielding and passionless as his new wife.

She would accept his money and would bear him a child without feeling anything. Had he a right to expect more? Colby had made it clear he would go on with his life as before. Wasn't that what he wanted all along? Wasn't that what made him accept Colby's preposterous scheme after he had insulted her? In God's name, he told himself, be content. But he wasn't.

Nevil turned and left the cabin.

He would never know that Colby had been watching him, wondering what strange thoughts were going through his mind.

When he returned an hour later, she lay prostrate, white, and exhausted, her face and clothes ringing wet.

Wordlessly, he went to the large ewer across the cabin, wet a towel, and came back to the bed. She hadn't the strength to send him away. Colby marveled at his gentleness. Her experience of men was jaundiced and limited to the few foolish young officers who had tried to curry favor with her father by attempting to court her. One had almost succeeded in attaching her interest, but that was soon over when wiser heads told him that Colonel Aden Mannering couldn't get himself promoted, much less press the hopeful expectations of a junior officer.

Even in the state she was in, Colby was forced to concede that not one man in a hundred would have submitted himself to such a nasty job as Nevil was doing now. It was a truth too disturbing to think about.

Nevil finished bathing Colby's face and neck in perfumed water and then set himself the task of opening an endless row of small pearl buttons. He swore at his first fumbled efforts. She raised her hand to stop him. It fell limply of its own weight.

"This is no time to worry about modesty," Nevil laughed, lifting the gown over her head. "I fancy I could always offer myself as a lady's maid if I lose my fortune."

Colby continued to protest, but in seconds he had her undressed and into a gossamer nightgown and under the covers. He tried, but failed, to keep his eyes from her breasts, as perfect as he had imagined, her creamy shoulders, and narrow waist. What a pity, he thought, that we did not meet under better circumstances. She was a woman any man would be enticed to folly. Might-have-beens were past thinking about, and this is an imperfect world. He lifted his shoulders and left the cabin. He needed a strong drink and the cold winds above.

Chapter 21

Paris was inhospitable, dark, and wet when they arrived at last. The skies opened and rain pelted the windows, fittingly, matched the mood within the frantically rocking coach.

Still weakened by seasickness, Colby slept most of the long way, and Nevil was glad. It enabled him to study her at leisure, something he hadn't been able to do before; nor, he was forced to admit, had he wanted to. She had kept to herself, and he was glad to postpone a few days the consummation of this poor excuse for a marriage.

The night on the yacht had been a terrible mistake. Holding her in his arms, her head heavy on his shoulder while he undressed her, had been far more disturbing than he wanted to recall. It had been far too long since any woman had seriously engaged his senses. There had been many women in his life before and after Gracia, but few had touched the core of him, whatever their charms. What a cruel irony if Colby, his bought-and-paid-for wife, turned him into a moonling. He wouldn't let that happen, and hardened his heart against her.

The coach suddenly careened crazily, throwing Colby across the interior and almost into Nevil's lap. He caught her up.

"What the bloody hell?" she cried, coming rudely awake to find herself in her husband's lap with his arms around her. "Take your hands off me."

Nevil sat her back on her side of the coach.

"So much for saving you from a nasty spill," he said, smiling witheringly. "I think we've broken an axle."

Colby looked down at her disheveled clothes, smoothed her traveling costume, and righted her hat before Nevil returned. She was sick at the idea of missing their entry into Paris, the appalling dampness that lowered her spirits. It all seemed an alarming omen of the weeks ahead. She couldn't bear to say, even in her mind, the word "honeymoon."

"We won't be able to continue, but we are not far from André's house. I sent a groom to fetch another coach."

"Am I to understand that we are not staying at a hotel, but someone's home?"

Nevil explained that André and his sister, Rita Barrault, were friends from childhood.

"I don't care who they are," she said fiercely. "I do not intend to subject myself to the prurient interest of friends of yours."

"For God's sake, Colby, stop being a child," he threw back at her. "The Barraults are the most cosmopolitan people you will ever meet, and the suite I usually occupy is a league away from the family quarters."

"You might have consulted me," she said testily, not at all sure she wasn't being unforgivingly difficult.

"I was quite certain you didn't give a damn where we stayed as long as I gave you a wide berth, and that, my dear, is what I intend to do."

Colby had to be content. At last he understood some of her feelings.

"But allow me to warn you once again, madam," Nevil said, his voice harsh. "As far as the Barraults and all my French friends are to know, this is not a contrived marriage. You will treat me adoringly, no matter what the public occasion and at whatever pain it causes you."

"You ask a lot of me," she said, smoothing the fine leather gloves that lay in her lap, her eyes directed at the rain beyond the windows. Colby knew she was behaving badly, but she couldn't stop herself. They'd made a bargain, and now she was trying to change it. And after he had ministered to her last night, too. She remembered little of what happened, but in the morning when she woke she was greatly disturbed to see that he had undressed her.

"I ask damn little of you, and will ask less in future," Nevil said, his anger feeding on itself. "I will not allow you to make a figure of fun of me. Most French marriages are as coldly pragmatic as ours, but they keep up appearances. You will do the same."

He sank back against the squabs, took a flask from his pocket, lit a cheroot, and waited none too happily for help to arrive. He was seething, and made no attempt to hide it. If there had been doubt, he knew now that his marriage was a terrible mistake. The future looked bleaker than ever. A curtain of discontent came down between them

The Hotel Barrault was a seventeenth century Parisian mansion of daunting proportions. Colby had no love for the ormolu inlaid furniture so dear to many of her countrymen. She much preferred the work of Sheraton and the Adams brothers. The heavy desks and bureaus vying with delicate, spindly-legged tables were the finest examples of their kind. Busts of male Barraults, sculpted to resemble ancient Roman senators, crowded every corner of the cavernous rooms. Clearly the family believed more was better, and the house was as near to a museum as any Colby would ever see.

In sharp contrast, André and his sister were as easy in their manners and demeanor as she could want. They greeted her with warm smiles and made her welcome. Standing on her toes, Rita took Colby in her arms and kissed her on both cheeks in the continental way.

"My dear, you are all I would have expected our dear Nevil to marry, and I greet you like a sister," the diminutive, dark-haired Frenchwoman said, surveying Colby approvingly from head to foot.

"It's my turn," André Barrault insisted, elbowing his sister away. "You always did have an eye for beauty, my dear boy."

Nevil blushed. he had been expecting an effusive reception, but when it came it was not to his liking. His displeasure with Colby was still too fresh, and he wanted to be done with it.

"Forgive me, ladies, but I must take André away," he said at once. "We have many things to talk about."

Rita took Colby by the hand to show her to their suite, and the men departed for André's study.

"Do I detect a note of reserve, my friend?" André asked, pouring large measures of brandy. "This is your wedding trip, is it not?"

"Of course, but actually it's more than that, André," Nevil said. "I'm here on an important errand for the Foreign Office."

"You English, no romance," André smiled. "L'amour. I much prefer the French way."

I would, too, Nevil told himself, with anyone less than the forbidding woman I'm leg-shackled to. He let the matter die there, and launched into the details of his mission.

"The FO hears that the Bonapartists are discontented, and violence may follow, designed to upset King Louis's rule," Nevil explained. "Have you heard anything?"

André left his chair and paced the large room, so simple and different from the rest of the house. Plain wood shelves of ledgers dealing with the huge Barrault family estates and business holdings dominated the masculine room.

"I hate politics, as you know, but one hears things, of course," he said at last. "Louis tries his best to placate all factions, but he is not always successful. Napoleon's followers will not be content forever and let him get on with it."

Nevil knew André well enough to know his friend would not stand on the sidelines and let his beloved France fall without a struggle. The Barraults had been pillars of the ancient regime and welcomed the Bourbons back with open arms. André's father and grandfather had seen the handwriting on the wall, and before the revolution had spirited the family and many of their treasures in a diversionary move to England. André and Nevil had met at school and forged a friendship that time and distance had never weakened.

"What have you heard, André?" Nevil asked, returning to the matter most pressing on him. "London is anxious for peace and stability. Is Louis in danger?"

"They would be crazy to touch him," André replied, but topped up their drinks before going to his desk. He pulled out some papers. "Read these before dinner, if you can keep your hands off that charming wife of yours."

Always irreverent where women were concerned, Nevil chose not to take offense. Memories of much whoring and carousing lay between them.

"You're an incurable romantic, André," Nevil said, rising.

André did not like the sound or look of his friend. Englishman or not, no man with a woman who looked like Colby would share his honeymoon with politics.

Rita Barrault gave Colby a quick tour of the house before taking her to the rooms she was to share with Nevil. The bedroom was as lofty and heavily furnished as the reception rooms below. A huge, richly carved bed with a crimson-and-gold velvet tester took over the room.

Colby stopped, terrified by the size of it and all it promised that night. She kept her eyes away, covering her distress with extravagant compliments about the accommodations. Colby prayed that she wasn't giving herself away.

The shrewd Frenchwoman saw enough to feel pity for her new friend. If she wasn't mistaken, Colby had all the earmarks of the reluctant virgin bride, dreading the marriage bed. Her Gallic love of romance and physical love stirred in her breast. Anyone lucky enough to capture Nevil Browning must be mad to shy away from the scene of all the delights such a man could offer. My child, you will feel differently in the morning, and if you don't, too bad of you!

With the least encouragement Rita would have jumped at the chance to trade places with Colby. She had nursed a secret *tendre* for the tall, blond Englishman from the moment André had brought him home. Fortunately, Pierre Faberge had come into her life when the Barraults returned to Paris, and Nevil was pushed to a corner of her heart. Since Pierre's death in a carriage accident a year after their marriage, Rita had known many men, but nothing to compare with her husband or Nevil. Life was strange indeed, and she sighed prodigiously.

"I'm not tiring you, Countess?"

"I am not at all fatigued, and we have agreed on first names, remember?" Rita said, recovering from her memories. "But I fail as André's hostess. You must be weary from that horrible voyage. What could Nevil have been thinking to subject you to it, and to keep you on the road since dawn was unthinkable."

"He is a famous sailor and does not understand mere mortals who sicken at the sight of rough water," Colby shivered. "The second mate told me he was like a Viking, standing at the rail all night when even the captain took to his cabin."

Rita didn't doubt it. André had told her that Nevil's army friends described him as the calmest of English officers throughout the war, rallying his men against withering fire as if he were on the hunting field. It took Badajoz to defeat him, Badajoz and the she-devil, Gracia Alvarez, Rita reminded herself. Could Colby overcome the ravages of war and Gracia? I could, the little Frenchwoman laughed in answer.

"And now I shall leave you and wrest Nevil from André and send him to you," Rita said with a lascivious look. "You must be perishing for the sight of him."

This time Colby's fears and reluctance were so apparent that Rita was sorry for her. She was deeply worried about the Brownings.

Dinner was an intimate affair with only two additional guests. Colonel and Mrs. Sherrod Marrow were distant relatives of Nevil's and old friends of the Barraults. Adele Marrow was a small, handsome woman, content to live in her husband's capacious shadow. He was inordinately tall and stout, the sort of man who blossomed in society, reveling in the best foods and wines and the company of the rich and infamous. The Marrows made no secret of their endless pursuit of public pleasure, and this, plus a large fortune, had made them welcome everywhere in the years since they had settled in Paris.

Nevil was greatly obliged to his cousins for making it unnecessary for him to contribute much to the dinner conversation. Marrow was a practiced raconteur and went on endlessly, and that enabled Nevil to go over the inexplicable events that had happened earlier in the evening.

His few feeble attempts to span the coldness existing between Colby and himself before dinner had been awkward and unsuccessful. Nevil blamed himself. As commodious as the suite was, with separate dressing rooms and anterooms, their dissatisfaction with each other still seemed to loom like an army of intruders.

"The Barraults are very taken with you." Dressed and waiting to take Colby down to dinner, Nevil had wandered into the bedroom.

"I like them very much." She would have said more, but the words died in her throat.

Nevil had forgone mourning clothes just before the wedding at his mother's insistence, and now, dressed in a burgundy velvet coat with gleaming white linen, he seemed to take over the room.

As he walked toward her, offering his arm, she wanted to shrink into a corner. Her breath came unevenly, her heart pounded, and all she could think of was that she was married to the handsomest man she'd ever seen. More than that, her body began telling its own story. A rush of heat traveled up her legs and across her belly, and to her horror she had to sink onto the bed, momentarily unable to stand. Realizing what she was doing, she shot off the bed and stood, shaking in every limb.

"Are you all right?" Nevil asked, crossing the room in a few long strides to catch her if she fell. She pushed his hands away roughly.

The thought of what was expected of her in the bed later that night was sending her mind in all directions like a rocket, and the last thing she could have endured at that moment was the feel of his touch.

But Nevil understood none of this, either then or at the very moment that his cousin was engaging Colby in conversation at the dinner table.

"My dear Lady Colby, how bad that you did not know Paris after Napoleon," the colonel was saying. "So untamed. So much drama. Duels were fought every day, and one Irishman in the Bourbonist Garde du Corps killed nine of his opponents in one year."

"Really, Sherrod, the ladies," his wife protested mildly.

"Really, Adele, Colby was raised on military posts. She understands stupid soldiers," Rita Barrault pointed out. "What was terrible to me was that all concerned went from the dueling grounds in the Bois de Boulogne to Toroni's for breakfast."

"Quite so," the colonel added. "A room was set apart for the most outrageous champagne repasts after each duel."

"You miss the Paris of five years ago?" André looked at him mischievously. "I remember well a dissertation of yours on the addled harridans of Faubourg St. Germain."

"Was that before or after they took you to their bosoms, dear cousin?" Nevil interposed good-naturedly.

"You can be sure it was before, Nevil," Mrs. Marrow laughed She was not always the dutiful wife.

"I really don't think we should speak so disparagingly of the old women of the ancien régime before our hosts," Colonel Marrow protested. "After all, André and Rita are related to many of them."

"Nonsense, Sherrod, I abhor them. They never forgave my father for being a liberal and for fleeing France successfully before the revolution." André smiled triumphantly.

Rita Faberge, who had decided to take Colby under her wing, started at that moment. She explained that with the restoration of the Bourbons, large sums were conferred on emigrés who had lost their money or estates for their devotion to the royal family. The contempt and disgust they felt for anyone who did not belong to their circle, Rita explained, was monumental.

"They are a criminally ugly lot, and their damnable pride, exclusiveness, and narrow-minded ignorance is legendary," Rita said as the others nodded.

"Quite so, my dear Rita," Mrs. Marrow interposed. "But when one was admitted to their circle, one was treated like a spoiled child, petted and flattered more than was good for one. Isn't that true, Sherrod."

The colonel spluttered, as the others laughed. Rita Faberge rose to her feet.

"I think perhaps it is time for the ladies to withdraw," she said. "André, please remember it has been a long day for the Brownings."

Chapter 22

With an effort of will that bordered on genius, Colby had dismissed her maid as soon as she came into the room, undressed, and fumbled with what seemed an army of small pearl buttons with shaking fingers without once looking over at the bed.

She went to the tall windows overlooking the garden below, now in almost total darkness except for a faint light coming from a ground floor room off to the side, trying to find solace of some kind for the night ahead. When she turned around, Nevil was entering from his dressing room carrying an ornate silver tray with decanter and glasses. He was wearing a richly brocaded robe, and dominated everything around him. She had not known he had returned, and started at the sight of him.

He put the tray on a table at the side of the bed and began pouring the brandy.

"I found a door to my dressing room further down the corridor," he said, his voice not quite achieving the even tenor he wanted. "I appropriated this from a young footman I suspect was on a mission of his own. Do you think the Barraults will mind?"

"I don't know," Colby replied, her voice barely above a whisper.

"Well, I've done the deed, and I think they will understand." He offered her a glass, surprised to see that Colby was frightened, her eyes lost and welling with tears like a child. This was a different Colby from all the others she had shown him. Gone was the sureness, the cold, hurtful woman he thought he

knew. It struck him, and not for the first time, that he rather
enjoyed jousting with that Colby.

"We can postpone this night," he said, moved by her terrors,
and wanting to give her time to gather her composure.

Colby took the glass, drank deeply, and returned it to him.
She threw him a wicked glance.

"Unpleasantness postponed is still unpleasantness," she
said, and walked to the bed like one on the way to a hanging.
She loosened her robe and climbed into bed, for all the world a
sacrificial lamb.

If Colby had spent years calculating a way to offend Nevil
beyond permission, she had succeeded admirably. It was in
just such a voice, in almost the same words, that Gracia Alvarez had spurned him when he had come back to her seeking
succor and love. With Gracia he had turned on his heels and
fled. Not this time. The stakes were different, and he was a different man.

Nevil tore off his robe and nightshirt, leaving them to fall
against the side of the bed. He blew out the light and arrived
full length on top of her, his long, lean body a match for hers
in every way.

Colby lay rigid and unfeeling, as he ran his hands along the
sides of her neck, his thumbs pressing lightly against her
throat, a warning of sorts. His breath was quick, almost a hiss.
Soon one hand moved up the nape of her neck, capturing thick
strands of hair, bringing her face closer to his. He forced her
lips open and began a rhythmic search of her mouth.

He arched slightly as his other hand moved sinuously between them, pulling away her silken nightdress until it wound
its way between her legs, and began exploring the core of her.

Colby cursed her wayward body, fighting a duet of rising,
maddening sensations and exploding barriers she never knew
existed and which she wasn't sure she wanted to escape. All
she knew was that she was angry with herself and this man
who was bringing her womanhood alive. She felt raw, vulnera-
ble, and all too human.

Nevil rejoiced at the way her body came convulsively alive
beneath him, and an excitement he had thought long dead ig-
nited. What had begun as a cold, calculated exercise to as-

suage his ego and to wound and dominate this woman who drove him mad had turned into exquisite passion meeting exulting passion he'd never experienced with any woman.

Colby caught fire, damned the consequences, and rose with him in waves of hunger, writhing beneath him like a wanton, but caring little for the sheer abandon of it. She wanted to moan, to cry, to laugh, anything that would give voice to this release she felt, but she had given away too much already.

Reason at last claimed Colby's mind. She willed her body to retreat soon after he climaxed. She bucked and rolled away, turning her back on him. He had won the night, but not her heart, Colby consoled herself.

"You are magnificent," he whispered, his breath and body slowly returning to normal, taking her in his arms.

Colby wrenched away, pulling the blankets over her naked breasts. "I hate you."

"You couldn't hate me and make love as we did."

"Animals do it all the time," she said, trying not to remember the heights he'd brought her to, the singing of her body.

"Please, Colby," Nevil said gently, reaching for her again. "It's nerves. Women often feel strange after they've made love for the first time."

Colby leapt out of bed, the covers dropping away. In the moonlight Nevil saw her breasts high and pointed, the nipples still hard and dark. She was more womanly, more achingly beautiful than before, and Nevil felt himself harden with need of her.

"Get back into bed. You're blue with cold," Nevil's voice was tight with desire. "Let me hold you."

"Don't you understand?" Colby screamed. "What happened just now was an aberration that will not be repeated."

Nevil was stunned. Once again he had been deceived by his loins. First Gracia; now Colby. Nevil's anger turned in him like a knife.

What a bloody fool I am. I dared to hope that the volcanic fire that rose between us just now meant something. For a few wonderful moments he had been deluded into thinking that he and Colby might after all be able to deal together as lovers and friends. He rose from the bed and slipped on his dressing gown.

"There will be as many repetitions of tonight as needed for you to have my child," Nevil said, his voice as emotionless as he could make it. "After that, you can go to hell. I wouldn't touch you with a barge pole."

Colby returned to bed as soon as the door to the dressing room closed. Her body ached in ways and places that weren't in the least unpleasurable. She felt drained, glad that the matter of her virginity was at last behind her. And Nevil would never again doubt her feelings for him and their future.

But why, in God's name, am I suddenly so unhappy. Tears like acid overflowed her pillow, and sobs she could not contain escaped at will.

Nevil lay stretched out on the small bed in his dressing room, smoking a cheroot, a balloon glass brimming with brandy precariously perched on his chest. His wrath knew no bounds. He called himself every kind of dupe, thought of divorcing her, reneging on their agreement, anything to erase her from his life.

But he knew he would do none of these things. He had no right to expect Colby to change toward him in any way just because their bodies shared a few moments of heaven. In that she is more honest than I am. She may have done many things that drove him to distraction, but she hadn't yet lied to him and did not fool herself, as he did. For all her inexperience, Colby knew, he conceded, that passion could not bring love where none existed.

Nevil sat up. He thought he heard sobs coming from Colby's room, but dismissed the idea at once. Hadn't she given him every indication that she wasn't a woman for maidenly tears?

Chapter 23

Colby woke an hour after dawn, cold and cramped in the same position in which she had cried herself to sleep. She went to the window, opened it, and looked out to see Paris coming to life, smoke pluming from roofs across the city, wagon wheels screaming under the weight of food from the farms outside the city. The cries of woodsellers and chimney sweeps rose to her on air clear and cold.

Colby's maid was tidying the dressing room and heard the noise. "My lady, you will catch your death." She pulled Colby toward the bed, trying to keep from staring at the wild disarray among the bed linen. Ilene Merl was a lusty, irreverent country girl, and the state of the bed did her heart good. It told her that her employers had been profitably occupied. She was not too pleased that there was no sign of the master. But the rich were like that, too many rooms in which to sleep, even on the honeymoon night.

Colby watched her Ilene's eyes widen and knew the reason. Nothing would allow Colby to reenter the bed, and she made for the dressing room, Ilene in pursuit.

"My lady, surely you are going back to bed?"

"I am not, and I want you to see that a horse is saddled for me and waiting at the door within the hour."

Ilene would have protested, but in the few weeks of her service she had learned when and when not to argue with her mistress.

Colby was at the door of the Barrault mansion at the hour dressed in a beautifully fashioned blue riding costume, one of four that Lady Miriam and Lady Barbara had insisted she order for her trousseau. Colby had argued against the extravagance, but was glad now that she had been overruled. The young groom and stable hand awaiting her arrival were, even for Frenchmen, beside themselves with unspoken admiration.

The groom stood at the head of a handsome, spirited chestnut. With the lightest touch he helped her into the saddle and ran back to mount his own.

Colby would have preferred to ride alone, but she knew that would have created a stir. She longed for her brothers and aunt and the sight of Brawleigh more than ever. With them and the land she loved over everything, she could be herself, and propriety could go hang. She waited for the groom to lead the way.

"If my lady pleases, I see you are most comfortable with Wildrose, and I suggest a brisk canter in the Bois de Boulogne," he said in heavily accented English.

Colby replied in flawless French and then asked the man his name.

"John."

"That is not a very French name," she laughed.

"All French grooms, no matter what their real names, prefer to be called John. The reason is lost in history," the groom explained.

They rode companionably through the streets, fast crowding with men on their way to work and housewives and servants seeking the freshest viands Paris had to offer.

Traversing the city—she asked John to take the long way to the Bois—the contrast between the rich district where the Barraults lived and where the poor existed was vast. Mansions and well-paved streets abounded, and signs of great improvements were everywhere, but not far away she saw crowded, fetid streets with open drains, crooked, narrow houses leaning against each other. Paris was not unlike London, but together they were far better than the major cities of India she had seen when she was growing up.

Nevil bathed and dressed hours after Colby left the house. He had slept fitfully and woke as soon as his valet opened the door. If the man was shocked to find his master not only sleeping alone, but in the dressing room, he was too well trained to show it.

"Billings, please see that her ladyship is told when she rises that I desire to speak with her in the small red reception room below."

"Lady Colby has not returned from her early morning ride," Billings said.

Browning turned ashen. What fresh outrage was this untamable woman planning for him?

"That's all right then," Nevil said, leaving the room. "I'll see her on her return."

Billings was not deceived for a moment. Nevil was furious, and the servant commiserated with him, for Lady Browning's unorthodox behavior that morning was the talk of the French upper servants' hall. What kind of bride deserts her marriage bed so early in the morning? No red-blooded Parisian husband would allow such a breach, they went on at breakfast, making the Browning servants the butt of their jokes.

Billings, a bachelor, and likely to remain so, had no suitable reply and was, if the truth were told, disappointed in his master. In his years with Lord Browning, lady loves fought to stay in his bed. But then how many Colby Brownings could there be? From the first, he had known she would never be a complacent wife, and he clapped his hands together, waiting for the fireworks he knew must surely come.

Nevil descended to the dining room, where André waited for him. No one knew better than he that a properly run French household of the higher order was always a mine of intrigue. French servants especially loved everything about love, and nothing in that line ever went unnoticed.

André was given the state of the Browning marriage with his early morning chocolate. He ached for his friend, but was too urbane to show it.

"I am arranging a meeting with several men you must talk with," André said smoothly. "Rita has promised to take care of Colby."

Nevil nodded and played with his breakfast.

"Have you any thoughts about where we must look for the

danger to the king?" he asked, glad to put all thought of Colby
to the back of his mind.

"I have a few ideas, although the threat can come from any
quarter," André said dolefully. "We must see what my friends
have to say."

They were about to leave the table when Colby arrived like
a whirlwind, her hat and veil trailing behind, her marvelously
waving raven hair, undone by the wind and the hand she ran
through it carelessly. She was panting for breath, her breasts
heaving against the heavy wool of her riding coat in such a
way as to shatter the calm of a statue. And André, Nevil, and
the male servants in the room were not made of stone.

"*Mon Dieu,*" André said so low no one heard. She's twice
the woman she was yesterday. For all his vaunted amorous ad-
ventures, the Frenchman was at a loss to remember the last
time any woman had bowled him over this way.

He no longer felt sorry for Nevil. If she was a perverse wife,
she was at least not an ordinary one. André dismissed her
heretical behavior, leaving her marriage bed at dawn, as something only an Amazon Englishwoman would attempt. He was
not partial to English beauties, preferring demure, pliant, Gallic ladies practiced in ways to pleasure a man. But if Nevil
were not Nevil, André laughed to himself, I might have run
him a race for her.

"I am starving," Colby announced, taking bread from the
sideboard before offering her cheek to Nevil for a kiss. Startled, he obliged, hiding his consternation admirably. I'm getting good at that, he told himself ruefully.

If she had decided to be the loving bride before their host,
he would play his part as well. He hated the charade she was
putting him to, but the truth of the matter was that her cold
cheek, her lilac scent lingered on his lips. Damn her. He
wasn't going to allow her to toy with him, giving and taking
herself away, no matter that he could not get the thought of her
out of his head and the feel of her out of his body.

At her insistence, the butler served Colby a heaping plate of
food, which she polished off like a field hand. André had
never seen a woman tear into food with such relish, and he
could not help staring.

"I am, after all, a farmer, and proud of it," Colby volunteered, grinning. "My ride was invigorating, and your Paris is wonderful."

"I cannot take you on an extended view of the city today, but perhaps tomorrow," Nevil offered.

"Don't bother," she said airily. "If André will allow me the use of a carriage and that nice groom, John, who is a famous guide, I shall be happy to explore the city on my own."

How queer things are here, André thought, sensing a current of feeling between them he could not read. He must talk to Rita. She would know what to make of it.

"I have many carriages, my dear," André said. "I am sure my sister will be enchanted to show you all of Paris. She knows it better than most, I assure you."

"And, of course, there are always the jewelry shops to visit," Nevil interposed, attempting to play the compliant husband, a role that did not suit him. But he had no alternative. His pride would not allow him to show he was upset, and his manners were too ingrained to tear at his wife in public as she deserved.

"I am bored by jewelry," Colby drawled.

Colby was playing the enfant terrible to the hilt, enjoying her husband's displeasure, and she didn't want to think beyond the moment. All she wanted was to hurt Nevil for something too nebulous to give a name. Much as she wanted to deny it, she knew it had all to do with the time they had shared in bed the night before. She shivered. Some things were not to be examined too closely.

"I would much rather see the latest farming tools and bring back some wheat seed," Colby said lightly. The rigid, disapproving look on Nevil's face was all she could ask for. He would have to learn to tread carefully around her.

"How original, my dear," André replied suavely. "I shall see that all men of Paris know of your existence, and you will set a new fashion."

"My wife," Nevil said, hurrying Colby out of the room, "likes to make mischief. It shall be my first task to teach her that not every clever thought she has needs to be aired in public."

André followed them out of the dining room, and the men agreed to meet later. He watched his guests ascend the stairs to their rooms, not happy for either of them. He was grateful that he did not have to deal with such a wife after all.

Nevil was in a towering rage when he opened the door of their suite and waited for her to enter.

"If it weren't for the job of work I have to do here for Tarn Maitland, I would frog march you to the nearest boat and ship you back to England." Browning paused for breath. "God help me, but I need to be seen as a simpering idiot on his honeymoon, and I am tied to you until I am finished."

Of all the things she'd expected him to say to her—and she knew she deserved a setdown—the thought that Nevil was involved in some intrigue delighted her. Colby was in no doubt that anything having to do with Maitland had to be exciting adventure.

"What sort of work?" Her interest was piqued, and she didn't care that it showed.

"If you promise to behave, you can have all the freedom you seem to crave," Nevil went on, ignoring her question. "If you feel this overwhelming compulsion once again to make a bloody laughingstock of me in public, I shall not hesitate to keep you locked up in this room."

She knew it wasn't an empty threat. In all the many moods she had seen him, this one was new. Her image of Nevil Browning as a flamboyant London hedonist underwent tidal changes from day to day. Would she ever really know this strange man she had married? It had been easy until now to keep her scorn at the boiling point for a fashionable rounder, but that picture kept changing. How could she ever forget Nevil's good humor while he bathed her face and held the sick pail during the voyage from Dover?

"Do you understand me, madam?" Nevil asked, demanding her attention.

"I will agree to be good, if you tell me what you are doing for Captain Maitland," she challenged him, not about to give in too easily.

"Not a hope!" he stormed. "You, who are quite capable of

deciding to score one over me for any fractious reason, would think nothing of making my mission the talk of Paris."

"Never!" Colby was stung by the idea that she could not be trusted.

"Even for the child you promised me," he said, his eyes narrowing, "I will not allow you to ridicule me ever again."

Colby was speechless. Was he describing her aright? Had she become a harpy, someone she couldn't recognize? She knew she had shown Nevil her worst side to pay him off for the way he had hurt her. Yet she didn't want to admit that she had fled that morning to make him look foolish. She knew the servants would gossip, knew André and Rita would learn that she left the house at an ungodly hour, when she was supposed to be in her new husband's sheltering arms. I made too good a job of it. She wasn't quite as proud of herself as she had been. His face when she arrived at the dining room, disheveled and triumphant, told her that she had succeeded in embarrassing him. And not content with that, she had gone on to be outrageously impertinent before André. Now all that was proving a less than perfect victory.

"Madam, you have tried my patience enough," she heard Nevil say as he headed for the door. "Remember, if you will not bend that stiff neck of yours, I will confine you to this room for the rest of our stay, which, I have decided, will not be a long one. I promise you."

He turned to look at her. She was standing at the window with her back to him, weighing his threat. Confined to one room, albeit even one as luxurious as this, would devastate her, especially with tantalizing Paris beckoning just beyond the window. She was trying to decide how to propose a truce without seeming to apologize, when someone knocked on the door.

The dilemma was resolved by a footman, who came with an invitation for Colby to join Rita at her house, which connected with the Barrault mansion through the garden.

"Her ladyship will join Countess Faberge in a few moments," Nevil announced, closing the door on the man.

"I do not intend to impose our mutual unhappiness on the Barraults or anyone else," Nevil said, weighing his words. He, too, did not want to seem to be retreating. "If you can control that rapier tongue of yours around Rita and André and stay out of my way, you can be as free as you like."

Colby's heart soared. The thought of sitting in the room with nothing to do except face the truth of her intransigence was too overwhelming. She nodded agreement, and left the room at his side.

Chapter 24

The maisonette Rita Faberge occupied was a gemlike doll-house. The Hotel Barrault was all stiff and glitteringly prized Louis XIV. Rita's little house was fitted with exquisite painted country furniture, and masses of flowers in huge Chinese vases and brass buckets were everywhere.

Colby felt at home immediately. Everything spoke to her of the country. Waiting to be summoned to Rita's boudoir, Colby roamed the drawing room thinking of similar ways to decorate at Brawleigh.

With the first monies that Nevil had given her, she'd arranged to settle her mother in Bath. Meanwhile, Colby sent home plans of all the improvements she planned for Brawleigh and her tenants. She would have all the money she needed to fulfill her ambitions for the boys. The thought of home restored Colby to the heights of optimism, and she was all smiles when a fat maid came to fetch her.

Rita's boudoir and bedroom occupied the second floor of the house. Every wall, every carpet, all the linen and silk draperies and chair coverings were graduated shades of yellow. Reigning over the sunburst was Rita Faberge, lying like a mythical temptress, purring over a bed overflowing with letters, books, baskets of fruit, discarded clothes, wigs, and a tray with half-eaten breakfast. The bed was enormous and took up most of the center of the room. Sharing it was an almost nude, supremely bored young man not more than eighteen, a sheet decorously hiding his endowments.

Taken aback, Colby did not know where to look.

"André tells me the marriage bed suits you, *mon petit*

chou," Rita laughed approvingly. "Of course, he is right. She is glorious, isn't she, Perri?"

Colby blushed, feeling like a milkmaid. She was no match for Rita's cool mastery of such moments, and wished she could leave the hot, overstuffed, sweetly perfumed room before making a cake of herself.

"Forgive me, my love." Seeing Colby's confusion, Rita was at last mildly contrite. "How stupid of me. I forget. The British love to make love; they don't like to talk about it."

Indeed, Rita was right. Idiot that I am, I liked last night much more than I wanted to, but I'll be damned if I'll tell you, or anyone, particularly a tall, too handsome, too broad-shouldered Celt across the garden, who is not at all happy with me at this moment.

"I merely came to bid you a good morning," Colby said when she could trust her voice. No longer able to ignore the young man and his rude activities with Rita under the thin coverlet, she needed to get away quickly. "Now if you don't mind, I think I shall change and take a carriage to Versailles."

"Perri has written an epic for me," Rita said, waving a sheaf of dirty foolscap and laughing at Colby's obvious discomfort. "Stay and hear it. He has many talents."

Colby promptly agreed that Perri was a gifted young man, but took her leave nonetheless. It was a constructive moment for her. She was convinced that Paris was a bit beyond what she liked to believe were even her unconventional standards. In fact, she was aghast at the scene she was forced to witness, but only hot coals would make her confess to a longing for the more staid precincts of England.

Chapter 25

Nevil and André dismissed their grooms and chose to walk in the clear, cold air of the late winter afternoon, going over the many avenues of intrigue opened to them during a long luncheon.

"My head is going in ten directions," Nevil said as they walked aimlessly. "Your friends had more theories than seemed possible, but no facts."

"I say there is no immediate danger, as your masters at Whitehall hear," the Frenchman insisted. "I think the liberals have had several victories lately, and the Bonapartists cannot muster enough support among the other anti-Bourbon factions for a concerted move against Louis."

"Perhaps, but that is dangerous thinking," Nevil said, heatedly. "You are looking for a major conspiracy mounted by Napoleon loyalists, but my instinct tells me otherwise. While Napoleon lives, anyone may want to avenge him."

"If you are thinking of an assassination, then how does one protect against madmen bent on mayhem in high places?" André asked, shrugging his narrow shoulders in the way that only the French can do so eloquently.

Nevil grinned. With that one cosmopolitan gesture André dismissed all the foibles of mankind.

"Forget politics for a moment, Nevil." André took him by the arm and directed him toward the Palais Royal. "I will show you how a true lover of women expresses his appreciation of the breed."

For Nevil the looming square of elegant buildings was like turning back a page of history five years. Recovering from his

wounds, unable to settle to anything, Nevil's friends had per-
suaded him to spend several months in Paris after the restoration of the Bourbons. Then the Palais Royal was a magnet for
English, Russian, Prussian, and Austrian officers and visitors
from all over the world. They'd come for many reasons, chief
among them to observe the diplomatic maneuvering of the Al-
lies. Of special interest were Wellington's efforts to soften
Blucher, who everyone knew would have devastated Paris if
he had his way.

The insanity of that time contrasted greatly with this day.
Then the streets had been rutted and dirty. Today all was
serene and clean.

"We shall select a bauble or two for my latest amour, petit
Marie, something for Rita's birthday in a few days, and something for the *charmante* Colby, yes?"

At times last night he would have gladly ransacked ten jewelry shops and laid their spoils on their marriage bed. But after
her infuriating behavior that morning, he had no heart for her
and no desire to watch André spend hours haggling over gems
with a merchant. It wasn't the first time Nevil had accompa-
nied him on such an expedition for his latest conquest. He
knew the drill too well.

"Speaking of my wife, André, when are you going to find
one?"

"In Colby, *mon ami*, you have taken the best prospect I've
seen in years," André said, executing a bow toward his friend.

"I agree, she is one in a million." Nevil kept his voice as
even as he could. He had no wish to sing his sad song for anyone, least of all André.

Together they visited a jewelry shop where a selection of diamonds, sapphires, rubies, pearls, and other perfections twin-
kled like stars against black velvet cloth. Nevil chose a rare
sixteenth century necklace and earrings of carved amethysts,
not unlike the color of Colby's eyes.

He would have preferred to buy a Browning bride diamonds
and emeralds, which were far more expensive, but he was not
about to leave himself open for her ridicule. He was in no
doubt that he would pay dearly for giving in to André's polite
blackmail as it was. To have showered her with gems that cost

a king's ransom would have brought down on him all the fires of hell.

Nevil waited none too patiently for André to finish his selections, and after an hour pulled him aside.

"André, I shall go upstairs to gamble a bit and try to recover the cost of my purchases," Nevil said, and made good his decision. He went to the gambling hell above, and in an hour walked out with laden pockets. André was not so lucky.

For most of the way to Versailles that afternoon, Colby was vexed with herself for the scenes she had provoked. She could no longer doubt that her behavior that morning was highly deplorable. The kaleidoscope of feelings and impressions that assailed her were not comfortable, and her confidence in herself was badly shaken.

She welcomed the long, slow exploration of Versailles with all the glories put in train by Louis XIV, the Sun King, in 1661. The cloud of mortification she felt for her actions lifted slowly. But she was young and hopeful enough to soon feel exhilarated to be in Paris alone, away from Nevil's brooding eyes, André's insouciance, and Rita, who she knew meant to shock her out of her British reserve.

Colby was able to laugh at Rita's exhibitionist young Perri, who she now realized had been determined to display his hold over his aging paramour in front of the priggish English intruder. In fact, Colby was rather proud of her quick recovery. With it came a little less awe of the worldly cynicism of her hosts. Perhaps even Paris would soon exert less of a blind, daunting hold over her. Truly free of the restraints she'd allowed to drag her down, Colby began to enjoy herself.

Colby credited Versailles for much of her lightness of heart. It seemed a very long time since she could remember feeling so free of the burdens she had assumed with her father's premature death. The undoubted beauty of the trees, manicured shrubbery, walks, gardens, fountains, and statuary was soothing to her badly frayed nerves.

She was particularly taken with the wide tapis vert, truly named the green carpet walk, that separated the grounds and led in dramatic fashion to the Grand Canal below. She watched as people of all stations promenaded in the chill, windless day, some attempting to walk blindfolded down to the canal between the vases and statues that bordered the great walk.

She meandered happily through formal avenues and squares and stopped to examine rows of yew trees cut into formal shapes. In the orangery, a charming old man pointed out numerous orange, lemon, citron, laurel, and pomegranate trees in vast tubs. She would have preferred to see them grow naturally, but French fashion decreed that they be uniformly trimmed.

"One orange tree is said to be five hundred years old," the man, who had become her self-appointed guide, told her walking among the trees.

She admired the flowers that bordered the orangery, white and yellow planted alternately, but the prettiest part of Versailles for Colby was the king's garden. It was modeled after the English house he lived in during his exile.

At dusk, Colby returned to Paris in a slight drizzle under a leaden sky, and regretted that it was less than a perfect ending for her day. But she had decided not to be unhappy. In a few weeks she would be able to leave for England, and that was to be her lodestar for whatever lay ahead.

Chapter 26

Colby longed for a hot bath and some sleep before the evening festivities, about which she hadn't a clue. She didn't care what they were, and fairly danced up the formidable stairway behind a footman.

She burst into her room to find the place hanging with clothes in such a variety of color as to set her back on her heels.

"The Countess Faberge wishes you to settle on one of these for the party tonight at the Duchesse de Remy," her maid imitated a French accent as she read the note aloud.

Ilene was pretty, well formed, and ambitious, and Colby enjoyed her irreverent humor immensely. Barbara Maitland had warned her that she was probably not doing Colby a favor. Ilene wore her independence like a medal from Prinny himself.

"Hell and damn," Colby fumed. "I won't accept clothes from anyone."

The maid ran to the door, looked out, and returned ashen. From the moment they met they had never quite managed to establish the traditional boundaries separating maid and mistress.

"You've done enough damage to Lord Browning's reputation this day. Don't make it worse tonight," Ilene said disapprovingly. "You are a woman of rank, Lady Browning, not a street urchin."

"This is none of your business, my girl." Colby's voice rose alarmingly.

"You wouldn't listen to advice from Lady Miriam or Lady

Barbara about ball gowns, remember?" Ilene stopped to draw breath. "The comtesse's dressmaker asked to see your clothes and pronounced them not grand enough for the parties you are going to attend while you are here."

"How dare she?" Colby might allow her own maid liberties, but this was beyond anything.

"I promised Lady Barbara I'd protect you, and that's what I'm doing. Try on these dresses," Ilene said blandly.

"You are too impertinent," Colby said angrily. "What if I choose to send you home?"

"I'll go, but you'll have no friend in this house to see to your interest and keep you from mischief." Ilene was cheeky, but Colby knew she was right and gave in grudgingly.

"Pick out something for me to wear, and leave me to my bath."

The Barrault party arrived at the imposing house near the Arc de Triomphe and were quickly surrounded by many of the overpainted, imperially grand dames and cranky old men of the aristocracy Colonel Marrow had told Colby about.

The ball was a terrible crush, the rooms too crowded and too hot despite the rain and cold outside. Colby was soon separated from the others. Grateful for the brief respite, she wandered alone after the mandatory introductions.

More importantly, she wanted to find a mirror in which to study the necklace and earrings that Nevil had given her just before they left the house.

"*Cherie,* how did you like Nevil's little gift?" André asked, seeking to make a little drama.

He had openly studied Colby's silver dress for signs of the amethysts, but she arrived at the drawing room without jewelry of any kind except the most ordinary wedding ring. With his huge wealth, André knew Nevil could have bathed his wife in jewelry. It seemed all apiece. The marriage was very odd and continually piqued his interest. There was nothing to stop him from asking Nevil the truth of things, but that would not be as much fun as learning it for himself.

André again asked about the necklace. Colby stared at Nevil. The last thing she wanted was a gift from him, much less a false display of marital affection in the presence of his friends.

"Really, André, is nothing sacred?" Nevil took the jeweler's box from his jacket and presented it to Colby. He had thought of giving them to her earlier, knowing that André would not fail to raise the subject, but he couldn't find the right moment or the words that were necessary. In truth, he was afraid she would refuse to have them and shame him again. As it was, Nevil was furious with Colby for not wearing the jewelry his mother gave her. His wife's eccentricities were not amusing.

Nevil had been right to fear Colby's response to his gift, but surrounded by Barraults and servants, she controlled herself. At Rita's insistence, Nevil put the necklace around Colby's neck, not at all pleased that his fingers shook with the touch of her. She was more and more intriguing and desirable, and much against his will he wanted to take her to bed every time he saw her.

Colby felt Nevil's fingers hot and fluttery like a butterfly wing around her neck, but never dreamt the cause. She suspected André's role in this purchase, and that made her even more uneasy.

But at the ball, at that moment, away from all of them, she was woman enough to want to see herself wearing the first jewels any man had ever given her. The family pieces that Lady Miriam had pressed on her would never be her own, and burned her skin in shame. She was convinced all Browning brides married for love. Her marriage was nothing. Eventually the amethysts would go the way of the heirlooms, back to a safe place somewhere. But for tonight she chose to believe she had a right to wear them. With luck she might be carrying a future Browning in her belly.

Colby slipped into a side room and sought out a mirror. To her astonishment, she found an odd pleasure running her fingers over the heavily carved stones made for some woman some man loved a long time ago. Her throat constricted with unshed tears. For the first time in her life, Colby wanted to be cosseted and petted like the woman of her imagination. She knew it was a dream without hope. She had never felt lovable. Too many young officers whom she had spurned none too gently, as well as her mother, had told her she was not, and she had come to believe it.

Colby couldn't understand what was happening to her. She was convinced that romantic notions had been knocked out of her in India, when she first began taking responsibility for her family, and she wanted it to remain so. She had a long, hard future ahead of her. Over the past few days she had made a resolve she meant to keep, no matter what the difficulties.

However long it took, whatever sacrifices it entailed, one day she would pay Nevil Browning every penny he gave her. Only then would she be released from the man who haunted her waking moments and embittered her dreams. She returned to the ball soon after, weary in every bone.

Colby was half asleep when she felt the bed sink under Nevil's weight. She had retired an hour earlier, trembling at the thought that she had sent Nevil away for good, and in agony that he might come to her insisting on his rights. She was riven in every way a woman could be.

She could not know that a similar war was going on in the room next door.

Nevil had roamed his dressing room trying to decide what to do. He wanted Colby as he hadn't wanted a woman since Gracia. In truth, he couldn't remember a woman who captivated him as she did. But she had told him she wanted no part of him, and he believed her, and he had spent the whole day in a frenzy of conflicted moods.

Nevil was the last man to see himself as a saint, far from it. He had drunk, whored, and cavorted with the best of them, but he had never forced himself on any woman, and he didn't want to begin now with Colby, of all women.

By heaven, she had tormented him from the first moment he had seen her. She was everything he thought he didn't want in a wife the few times he had even allowed himself to imagine what it would be like to be married. After Gracia he thought he disliked competitive, single-minded, combative females, and here he was languishing after a she-devil who put Gracia in the shade.

Nevil blew out the candle and tried to sleep, but his mind

dwelt too graphically on the face and body of the woman beyond. In seconds he was fully aroused. In that state he came to her bed.

It was a silent war they waged. Two magnificent bodies fighting for supremacy and gratification without word or gentle murmur, taking no prisoners, neither asking nor taking any quarter. They wanted it all on their own terms.

Nevil's mouth and hands and sex were all over her, taking away whatever breath she had, searching and finding those places where her womanhood dwelt undiscovered, unknown. She met him stroke for stroke, urgency for urgency, flame for flame, until there was nothing left to take or give, and they came away spent, breathless, unappeased. A truce of sorts.

Nevil was not going to make the same mistake he'd made the night before, presuming that because they made perfect love together it meant they could feel anything for each other. He knew love, the word, the feeling, and the unconquerable need for another were as foreign to her as any distant planet.

He left soon after.

This night Colby would not give in to tears. Much as she wanted to ask for a second chance to speak of her longings, her loneliness, her wish to be more than a carrier of his seed, she couldn't ask Nevil to stay. It would have meant surrendering herself, and that she would never do.

Chapter 27

Colby arrived at Rita's boudoir after another morning summons, determined that she would be as blasé as she could contrive.

Two weeks in Paris had added vastly to her knowledge of Continental life, even if she could not always approve of its form. The freedom with which wives and husbands and their lovers gloried in and displayed their liaisons in society no longer shocked her sensibilities. For that she could thank André and Rita, whose own highly volatile affairs were the subject of clinical discussion at every possible occasion. She knew such goings-on happened in England, but much more behind closed doors.

One night brother and sister found an old love of Rita's in the arms of André's current love. Only Nevil's quick intercession prevented a duel on the spot. It was a near thing, but later the Barraults treated the whole affair as a great joke.

She and Nevil had been wined and dine by what seemed the whole of French society, and when that source threatened to run its course, Colonel and Mrs. Marrow introduced them to others. In one of the few spontaneous exchanges between them, Nevil asked Colby how she was faring.

"If I have to stand for one more gown fitting or sit at one more indigestible dinner, I shall scream," she replied.

"I feel the same," he said, and then a shyness enveloped them, and they retreated.

Colby had reason to recall the meal of the previous evening, which had kept her awake a good part of the night.

"Colby, you are an angel to come so quickly."

Rita was half dressed, with a dressmaker, hairdresser, and assorted tradesmen with merchandise spread haphazardly around the room like an Indian bazaar. Everyone was nattering at full volume, and before long Colby had the makings of a headache.

"Amuse yourself, my dear. I shall throw them all out in a moment, and we can talk."

Colby fled into an adjacent room to get away from the din. It was one huge wardrobe, and she made a circuit of what a French lady of means had to have to be considered fashionably correct.

Not in the least interested in such matters—indeed, she couldn't wait to get back into her father's old army rig—Colby nevertheless was overwhelmed by Rita's needs. Dresses and gowns were too numerous to count, so she contented herself with smallclothes and the like. She counted fifty pairs of stockings of every color and elaborate decoration, including butterflies, Chinese dragons, and clocks.

Colby looked through drawers of cuffs, ruffles, one hundred chemises, and handkerchiefs. Petticoats were made of sprigged muslin, watered silk, taffeta, striped brocades shot in pigeon breast effects, and others she found indescribable. Rita's coats and capes spoke of the history of furs. Wearied by the inventory of female finery that could dress ten women, Colby wandered back to the boudoir.

"Rita, I must go. I have many errands," she pleaded. The room seemed filled with even more people than before. Rita's sense of time was atrocious, and, in fact, Colby needed to buy more gifts for the boys and her aunt.

"Allez vous," Rita demanded at last, and they all left at once. "Now, my darling Colby, let me see how adventurous you are," Rita said, dismissing her maid when she was dressed.

"That depends."

"Oh, you English, so cautious."

"Tell me what you want," Colby laughed. "I can see you are dying of excitement."

"I have learned what great things Nevil and André have been pursuing."

Colby's ears perked up. She had never been content with Nevil's refusal to trust her enough with knowledge of his mission. It had hurt deeply, and now she had a chance to satisfy her curiosity.

"Nevil has this mad idea that the king and the government are in some danger," Rita volunteered. "André and his friends have learned nothing, so I have decided that we shall help them. I want you to come with me to see my old love, the painter Gericault."

"Isn't he the one who does horses so well and painted 'The Raft of the Medusa'?"

"You are so fond of making yourself some kind of country maid, one doesn't realize you are very well informed," Rita taunted, steering her out of the room. "Theodore is not that well known abroad."

"Papa was most disturbed when the Medusa went down in the storm. The terrible desertion of the sailors by the officers and the cannibalism was a torment to him," Colby recalled. "He followed the disaster closely, so I was interested to hear Gericault's painting of the calamity made a commotion at the salon last year."

"Well, now you shall meet my darling Theodore," Rita said as they entered the carriage and were driven to his studio in the Rue des Martyrs.

"What has Gericault to do with Nevil's mission?" Colby asked.

"He is very much involved in the Bonapartist cause," Rita explained. "For a long time he was not concerned in politics, but Carle Vernet, his friend, is and has involved poor Theo."

They arrived soon after, and the young artist devoured Rita with his eyes. Now that she knew a little bit about such things, Colby was certain that the painter with very little encouragement would have taken Rita to bed there and then if she weren't present. She felt a third leg, and more, she envied Rita's easy bantering way with men. Only one man could ever mean anything to Colby, but she didn't want to think about that. She hastened to look at the paintings and sketches cheek by jowl around the walls. It wouldn't do for anyone to see the tears she could not stem.

Gericault was extravagantly welcoming, and Colby was happy to be in a Paris artist's studio at last. While Rita and Gericault talked of old times, she studied the man and his work. He was well dressed and barbered, so unlike most of the starving painters and writers she had seen in her solitary walks through the artists' quarter.

Rita had said Theo had inherited money and lived on a grand scale, buying racehorses and businesses, which she insisted he knew nothing about.

"How wonderful to see you. But what brings you here after so long?" Gericault asked as he found a sketch pad and began to draw a quick, sure study of Rita. "Does André still disapprove of me and my politics?"

"Since when did André's likes or dislikes stop me?" Rita glanced at Colby, distressed at the painter's perspicacity. "I came to show Lady Browning what a real artist is like. She knew all about 'The Raft.' Doesn't that impress you?"

Gericault was delighted, and Colby had to repeat everything she had told Rita.

At last there was nothing any of them could think of to say that would prolong the visit, and Rita silently appealed to Colby. To give her more time, Colby found two preliminary studies of heads, and Gericault told her they were sailors drawn for "The Raft." She insisted on buying them.

Escorting them to the carriage later, Gericault engaged them in the mildest pleasantries until he was about to turn them over to the groom.

"Rita, darling, tell me why you really came," the artist chuckled. "I am dying to know."

"You know me too well, *cheri*." Rita kissed him on the mouth. "Would you tell me if you knew of a plot against the monarchy?"

Gericault stepped back and looked at her, his eyes dark with instant fury.

"You should know I would never be a part of anything like that," he said and turned, leaving them standing on the street.

They rode in silence. Colby was appalled at Rita for sacrificing Nevil's work, but hated herself more because she was too cowardly to call her friend to task. Nevil would be beside himself, and it was all her fault. She should have refused all Rita's blandishments.

"I am still convinced something is afoot, and I will persevere." Rita recovered her spirits and urged the coachman on.

Colby threw up her hands. The woman was incorrigible, and she couldn't help thinking her wonderful all the same. But she hated to think what Nevil wold say when he learned of their foolhardy venture.

But later, when her conscience gave her no peace, Colby insisted on confronting Nevil and André in the drawing room, both uncomfortably costumed for the masked ball that night at the home of Comtesse Greffulhe.

Browning, dressed against his will in padded clothes to look like Henry VIII, was trying to smooth white hose over his muscled calves, while Barrault made a great show of looking like a sinister Emperor of the Turks in a splendid jeweled coat and turban.

Before Colby could persuade Rita to own to their indiscretion, she insisted that they show off their costumes. Colby obliged and paraded the room in a copy of a pre-Revolution gown with billowing panniers and powdered hair.

"Colby and I have had a very successful day today," Rita said at last, accepting a glass of wine from her brother. She was flaunting her matchless figure in an Albanian soldier's uniform modeled after the Phillips portrait of Lord Byron. She looked rakish in a mustache, pleated skirt, embroidered jacket, and cloth headdress, and she knew it. On her back she had pinned a sketch of the original portrait.

"Rita, tell them," Colby insisted, her nerves no longer able to stand the suspense.

"We learned that something is about to happen to the monarchy."

Nevil flew out of his chair.

"What are you talking about?"

Despite his glare, Rita went about gaily explaining their afternoon visit in all its detail.

"André, I hold you responsible for this breach," Nevil shouted. "It will be all over town before morning, and I shall be made to look like an idiot in Whitehall."

André took his sister by the arm and marched her out of the room.

"As for you, madame, why did you go along on this outrageous jaunt when I expressly told you I did not want you to know of my work?"

Colby could not think of anything to say that would not exacerbate her guilt. She didn't even try to put a good face on it. She'd known she should have dissuaded Rita from the expedition, but, in truth, she had been a willing collaborator until Gericault caught them out.

André returned before Nevil could go on haranguing her.

"I am convinced no harm has been done, Nevil," he said and ushered them out to the carriage that awaited them. "Gericault has no influence, and no one would take him into a cabal."

Nevil was still bitter, and except for introductions that could not be avoided, kept himself apart from his party most of the evening.

Colby pleaded a headache and found refuge in the library. Nevil had been unhappy with her often, but there was something about this night that made her particularly concerned. She was feeling sick and on the point of quietly leaving the ball when Rita came looking for her.

"You must come at once and see the enchanting Duchesse de Berri." Rita was beside herself; she loved royalty in all its forms.

Colby followed Rita to the ballroom. There Marie-Caroline and her husband Charles, the king's nephew and heir to the throne, were easily the most important guests and the center of attention. Even from a distance Colby could see the eldest daughter of the king of the two Sicilies was irrepressible. She dazzled as "Queen of the Middle Ages" in a cherry velvet dress with wide, slashed sleeves trimmed in ermine. A hat to match sat pertly on her shining blond hair.

Not long before the royal party left, the Barraults insisted that Colby and Nevil meet the duchesse. She was talking to the Duc Fitz-James. Earlier in the evening when they were introduced, he told Rita he was presenting small knives in imitation of the actor Posier, who gave knives to his daughters in the opera currently playing at the Porte St. Martin. Fitz-James and the actor were the rage of Paris for their histrionics. Fitz-James was presenting Marie-Caroline one of the knives as the Barrault party approached.

"What place in the heart should one strike?" they heard Fitz-James ask the duchesse, and everyone laughed. Everyone except Nevil, who turned on his heel and waited for them at the carriage.

"I didn't find Fitz-James's remark in the best of taste," Browning said as they took off for home.

"Really, my friend, you are getting quite grim," André said, irritated by Nevil's morbidity.

"If the Duc de Berri is the king's heir, why couldn't he be the target we have been looking for?" Browning asked.

"I hate to think you may be right," André said, suddenly catching Nevil's pessimism.

"Enough," Rita shouted. "You are making my skin crawl."

Colby thought of the lovely young woman looking adoringly at Charles de Berri, and a cold chill ran down her spine. She hated to think anything would happen to them.

Once home, André and Browning bade them good night to closet themselves in his office.

Hours later Nevil returned to his dressing room, still furious with Colby for abetting Rita in her rash interference. But it was never easy to forget that his wife was next door.

Colby waited for him for hours. It had become a ritual with her. She would promise to withhold herself, but when he slipped into bed, she forgot her resolve and met him halfway. But it was becoming harder and harder for her to suppress the ecstasy she felt, the need she had for him. She yearned to hold him in her arms and give release to the singing of her body. Words and sounds echoed in her mind, but never on her tongue. To lose her head and her heart would be to reveal too much. She wasn't prepared for that and never would be.

Colby buried her face in her arms and poured out her unhappiness, damning the day she ever saw him.

Chapter 28

Rita Faberge, her hair piled on top of her head, came to Colby's room a week later wearing a capacious cloak. A bewigged footman, weighed down with a large bag, arrived at her heels. Rita dismissed the man, and Ilene, whose eyes were as big as saucers, was sent away soon after.

"Now, *cherie,* out of bed. We have another adventure today," the Frenchwoman said, throwing off her cape to reveal the uniform of a captain in the French Army. She went to a mirror and placed an army cap on the top of her head.

"You're insane, and I will have no part in this," Colby protested.

Her friend laughed away her fears and brought out the uniform of a major in the same regiment.

"This is for you," Rita said and began tearing at Colby's nightclothes to hasten her into the uniform.

"I have taken Colonel Marrow into my confidence, and he will be here shortly."

"Nevil is still so angry with me, he hasn't come to my . . ." Colby's words trailed off. Fortunately, she saw that Rita was far too involved in her scheming to notice her near slip of the tongue.

Rita was perfectly aware of what Colby almost blurted out, but once her mind was made up to do something, she had no hesitation about using whatever weapons were at hand.

"Are you afraid of Nevil?" Rita Faberge asked contemptuously. Like her brother, she enjoyed domestic drama.

"Nonsense. I'll be ready in a tick."

Colonel Marrow was of two minds about escorting two ladies dressed as officers to a café near the Palais Royal.

"I assure you, Rita, I can learn all you need to know about André's machinations without all the fancy dress," he insisted.

"You don't know Rita, if you think she can be talked out of any idea that comes into that fertile head of hers." Colby was still skeptical.

Once having tried to dissuade them, Sherrod Marrow made no secret of his wish to be included in the scheming, but he still felt pressed to make some gentlemanly warning. "Now don't be at all shocked by the conversations you might hear and ruin your disguise."

"I am not so easily overturned, Sherrod," Rita protested, playfully slapping him on the sleeve of his elegant coat. "I think I make a perfect soldier."

"Officers don't strike other officers as if they were holding a fan," Colby laughed. "Such lapses worry me. One large gaffe, and we will be discovered and disgraced."

"No one will notice if you don't call attention to yourselves," Marrow advised, but he gave them each a cigar and a newspaper. "Here the crème de la crème of male society talk only of gambling and women. We'll come about."

The café was a dark room over a leather shop. Using an outside stairway, they were greeted with deafening noise. Colby's fear that anyone would see beyond their disguise was immediately eased, and she began to enjoy the escapade. Marrow led them to a table in the rear, past the counter at which a woman presided. She was extraordinarily endowed above the waist, a fact which she seemed delighted to reveal to her male clientele.

Colby fought against laughing aloud. Rita would have stopped to stare had not Colby pushed her, none too gently, forward.

Marrow ordered them cups of mocha and an ice for himself. Rita recognized most of the men present.

"Half are related to me."

"Precisely. Why would André choose this place for his meeting, when everyone he knows is here?" This had been worrying Colby from the beginning.

"It will save him time," Marrow replied. "Anyone who is anyone in Paris comes here at least once a day. If you want to know what's going on in Paris, someone here will tell you."

Colby was not at all certain of his logic. "Wouldn't that mitigate against privacy, if André and Nevil are seen here making plans or asking dangerous questions?"

"My dear girl, if you want to hide your intrigue, do it in the open. No one will suspect you."

Fifteen minutes later, André and Browning arrived, surveyed the vast room, greeted many, and joined a large table across the way. The conversation was animated, and Colby saw that no one paid André's party any special attention once they sat down.

Colby was suddenly afraid for Nevil. There was nothing about him that suggested the cold, cutthroat love of mystery and plots. She was remembering some of her father's men who courted danger as a sport and regarded infiltrating enemy lines, indulging in mad and hazardous exploits as a larky stroll down Piccadilly. She wasn't disparaging her husband's courage, she merely doubted his liking for the dark side of life. Perhaps Tarn Maitland knew better, and for a moment she would have to be content with that.

She couldn't keep her attention anywhere but on Nevil, who towered over his companions and, to her mind, was the handsomest man in the room. He was becoming an obsession. There in that crowded room she had finally admitted it to herself. Another night without him was unthinkable, and there lay disaster. She had to get away. She had to do it soon, very soon.

Rita had been trying to get Colby's attention from the time Nevil entered the room. She could not read all that her friend was going through, but as a woman whose heart had been broken with the regularity of the dawn rising, she recognized love gone wrong. Poor girl, the Frenchwoman thought, you need wise counsel.

A half hour later Marrow called for the bill. "Give me a few minutes, and then leave," he said, seeming more conspiratorial than André or Nevil. "My coachman has been instructed to take you nearby, and I will join you."

Rita and Colby protested, but he was adamant.

Jaunty and full of the success of their venture, Colby and Rita departed soon after and waited in the carriage.

"If you were in my regiment, I'd have you shot."

Colby and Rita jumped.

"You two are about as military as my hunting dog." It was Nevil, and behind stood a crestfallen Sherrod Marrow.

"How did you know?" Rita threw up her hands, deflated to have been found out.

"Your scent is very powerful, and as you were with Sherrod, I could hardly fail to look over at your table."

"There was no harm done," Colby cut in. "We were bored and wanted a revel, nothing more."

"I have heard about the café for years, and it seemed such different diversion to give Colby."

"I don't believe a word of it." Nevil said grimly. "This is dangerous work, and you are a threat to us."

"Perhaps if you told us what this is about, we would be content," Colby said defiantly.

Rita agreed, and with Colonel Marrow as an interested spectator, Nevil decided to tell them enough to slake their interest.

"On evidence we have collected, André and I have been able to convince some of his friends that the royal family is in imminent danger from a number of factions," he said, exasperated. "We are arranging unofficial protection whenever certain members of the family leave the Tuileries for the next few months."

"How marvelous," Rita shouted.

"Why can't we help you?" Colby asked excitedly. "No one would suspect two women like us."

Nevil appealed to Marrow to help him talk sense to them.

"They may be right, old boy."

"I'll talk to André," Browning said, not at all appeased.

"When do you and André start?" Colby asked.

Nevil told them they were to go to the opera that night, because someone knew that the de Berris were to be there.

"To be sure, Virginie Oreille, one of Charles's old mistresses, is to dance in the ballet of Les Noces de Gamacheo,"

Marrow told them. "He is very loyal, and Marie-Caroline is very tolerant."

"Then we go tonight!" Rita announced.

A thick fog, spreading cold and damp over Paris, greeted the Barrault party that evening as they left the house. The atmosphere in the carriage was not unlike the weather outside. Smothered in furs, Colby and Rita tried to make conversation, but the men were somber and unresponsive.

"You are like statues," Rita chided them. "Nothing will occur tonight. Too many people about. Let us enjoy the opera."

Colby tended to agree, but knowing that both men carried guns and were ready to use them at the least provocation, she could not lend herself to Rita's gaiety.

André was the most visibly distressed.

"This is a Frenchman's problem, not yours, Nevil." It was apparently an old argument, and Browning tried to stop him. "If something happens and it is learned that you are here for the Foreign Office, it could be construed that the English government was involved in an internal matter."

"You worry too much," Nevil said. "Only Sherrod and you three know why I am here. I can always say I am acting on my own."

Once again Colby found her heart heavy with concern for her husband's safety. And if all recent signs were true, the child she was carrying needed a father. She had kept the news to herself and intended to do so for as long as she could. A plan was taking shape in her mind, and it needed all her attention.

At seven-thirty the carriage approached the opera house at rue de Richelieu and rue Rameau.

"Nevil, please take the ladies in. I shall wait at the entrance to the royal box," André said and quickly disappeared.

Browning tried to go in his place, but his host would not listen.

Colby could not contain her excitement. This was to be her first experience of an opera, a longing she had had since she was a child. She loved music and had been taught by an Indian woman how to play the piano reasonably well. She had a lovely, untrained contralto and sang and played for her own amusement. Save for Matthew, who could sit and listen to her for hours, all the Mannerings were tone deaf.

Nevil's attention was with André, and he hurried the women inside. Colby was overwhelmed by the grandeur that unfolded before her like a fairy tale come true.

The opera house was huge and lit with more candles than Colby had ever seen in one place. The crescendo of noise, musicians preparing for the performance, and the glittering audience that greeted them as they made their way added to her pleasure. People she and Nevil had met at the various parties they had attended were extravagant in their greetings. The men bent low over her hand with compliments for the way she looked in a black gown, cut provocatively low, that revealed her rounded shoulders and flawless neck. It was one of six she had been forced to commission Rita's dressmakers and other couturiers to make for her at great haste for princely sums.

"I told you that dress would devastate," Rita remarked proudly.

"You are converting me to a frivolous spendthrift," Colby moaned. "I will have no use for these at home."

Rita looked at Colby for a long, uncomfortable moment while people buffeted them on all sides.

"Your husband is criminally rich and has a position to uphold," Rita said. "Make your marriage less of a battlefield."

Colby was taken aback. She had not given her friend credit for caring or noticing anything but her own affairs. She looked over at Nevil, besieged by some of the most beautiful women in Paris, and her heart went cold. He was warm and obliging in his gallantry, all smiles and compliments. But if he had noticed what she wore each night when they were wined and dined at one more sparkling gathering than the next, he gave her no sign. It seemed a long time since they had even looked at each other full in the face. This won't do, Colby told herself and concentrated on the reason for being at the opera. I cannot afford jealousy in my life.

At last they arrived at the Barrault family box, and Colby's glance immediately went in search of the Duc and Duchesse de Berri.

The royal box held only a few people, but Colby could imagine where Marie-Caroline would sit. Three light blue taffeta screens shielded the box from the heat of the footlights. Two armchairs of blue Utrecht velvet waited empty.

Two men and a woman came to talk with Rita, and Nevil chose that moment to make his excuses and join André. He found him standing in the shadows across from the sentinel guarding the private entrance to the royal box while the opera house manager paced back and forth nearby.

"Once I see Charles go in, we can leave," André said by way of greeting.

"See anything to worry you?" Nevil asked. André shook his head. A moment later they heard the rumble of several carriages in the distance.

Nevil's attention was drawn to a small, dark-haired man in a great coat, who seemed to be waiting for the arrival of the carriages as intently as they were.

"Do you see that fellow over there?"

André looked up, but dismissed the man at once.

At last the carriages arrived from the left led by an outrider in the livery of the royal family. They heard the manager shout importantly, "Present arms!" and guards poured out of the door of the opera house bearing rifles on their shoulders.

André went toward the carriages, which arrived smartly and stopped between the gray painted posts flanking the porch. Nevil and the man moved with him. Browning was close enough to see the stranger's flashing blue eyes staring without a flicker at the royal party. The man's face was pale with what seemed like extraordinary strain. Nevil felt unaccountably nervous.

A valet let down the stairs of the first carriage and opened the door. Charles de Berri emerged first, then turned to assist his wife. Together they led their party inside.

André with Nevil behind him went to join the Comte de Mesnard, who ordered the carriages to return at ten forty-five.

The comte and André shook hands, chatted for a moment, and parted. Their job was half done.

The two returned to the opera house through the main entrance, managed to find a drink, and then went to the Barrault box.

Colby did not notice their arrival, she was too wrapped up in the lilting music, glorious voices, and colorful scenery that made the night enchanting.

Nevil watched her, marveling at the changes he saw. In a few short weeks she had become an alluring, cosmopolitan woman. Every encounter with French society, who were high sticklers and prickly to a fault, every experience in magical Paris she greeted with charming enthusiasm.

The new Colby he saw emerge might often drive him to distraction, but he could no longer deny that the warmth she showed others was something he prayed would one day animate toward him. He knew he must do everything in his power to make her love him. But it wasn't going to be a simple matter. Too much hurt had formed to create a deep chasm between them.

She was in such contrast to the hard-faced, bored women he knew in Paris and among his own set in London. The rules of the game with women had always seemed so simple. Lavish money and false love, and they fell like tenpins. He wasn't proud of it, and it certainly hadn't prepared him for someone like Colby, who broke all the rules and yet ensnared him for life without even trying. Anything but.

Nevil's reverie was interrupted by the appearance of the duc and his wife just as the first of the three short operas was about to begin.

Colby could not take her eyes off the couple. It didn't seem possible that anyone wanted to harm the golden pair, and yet she felt an unease that equaled Nevil's.

In the first interval she took André aside and asked him about the duc.

"Since his marriage to a king's daughter, Charles has become a personage in his own right, but has no love for the king, which he does not hide," André explained at length. "He thinks Louis is too moderate and the army has too many Bonapartist sympathizers, and I agree. But he bullies the army and makes too many enemies."

Neither was aware that Nevil had been listening to their conversation.

"When are you going to talk to de Berri and tell him to increase his guard?" Nevil asked, making his presence known.

André nodded and left for the duc's box.

Left alone, the two were shy of making the first approach, and soon it was too late. Rita arrived with men on all sides, and the opera resumed.

At ten o'clock André returned and told them he had not been able to talk with Charles de Berri.

"I will see him after the performance," he whispered to Nevil.

An hour later, Rita took up her opera glasses and surveyed the audience, her glance alighting on the royal box.

"Charles is escorting Marie-Caroline out, André."

"Not to worry," said a man sitting next to Rita. "He has probably convinced her she's tired. After all, Virginie dances next, and we all know about Charles and his amours."

"And there is always the anteroom off the box"—André joined in the general laughter—"where he can show his appreciation of her dancing."

Too keyed up to remain for the rest of the performance, Nevil slipped out unnoticed by everyone save his wife. He quickly exited the opera house and huddled in his coat, walked around to the royal entrance at rue Rameau again just as the footmen greeted the Comte de Choiseul, who appeared ahead of the Duc. Without coat or hat, de Berri turned to see his wife emerge, followed by de Mesnard. She joined her husband, and both paused on the little porch to see the guard present arms. Marie-Caroline entered her carriage, and the steps were put up.

Nevil was close enough to hear the duc talk to his wife through the carriage door.

"Goodbye, Caroline," he said. "We shall see each other again soon."

Before the carriage moved, de Berri, shivering in the dampness, started to follow de Choiseul indoors. At that moment, the man Nevil had seen earlier in the evening darted between the sentry and the carriage and fell on de Berri with a knife.

Browning couldn't believe what he saw.

"There's a clumsy lout," he heard de Berri cry out.

"Mind what you are doing!" De Choiseul was pulling at the man's coat, but he eluded his grasp and made off in the direction of rue de Richelieu.

"Guards, after him," Nevil ordered.

"I have been assassinated. The man has killed me," de Berri moaned. "I am dead . . . I am holding the dagger!"

Three men took off after the attacker, and Nevil bent down to assist the wounded man.

The duchesse would not wait for the carriage steps to be let down. "I order you to let me go," she screamed, pulling away from her lady-in-waiting, who tried to hold her back. Marie-Caroline jumped and fell at her husband's side, crying in fright.

"Come, my Caroline, let me die in your arms," de Berri begged.

With the help of Browning and others, the duc insisted on getting to his feet. Leaning against a post and with unbelievable strength, he pulled the knife out of his chest. Nevil begged him not to, but he persisted. It was a sharp blade with a crude wooden handle and reminded Nevil of tools he had seen in his own stable.

Nevil pleaded with Marie-Caroline and her lady-in-waiting, their pretty dresses stained with blood, to wait for a doctor, but they pushed him aside and assisted Charles to a red bench inside the guards' room.

Again he protested, but Mesnard would not listen and began unbuttoning de Berri's green coat and yellow waistcoat. Blood from the terrible wound gushed out.

"I am dead," Charles panted. "A priest, quickly."

Nevil was elbowed aside and for the first time could assess his surroundings. It was a scene he would never forget. A bishop arrived and began reciting prayers in Latin. The duchesse emitted heartbreaking screams and lamentations, which, when mixed with the lively music in the gala performance beyond, seemed to him something no madhouse had ever witnessed. No one had bothered to call a halt to the performance.

"Doctors are on the way," someone shouted, and Nevil thought it best to leave. He turned, and there was André. He and Colby were supporting Rita between them. Near collapse and unable to stand, she nevertheless refused to leave.

"What happened?" André whispered, tears running down his face.

Nevil gave him a summary of the stabbing.

"Nevil, are you hurt?" It was Colby. She had just seen the blood on his clothes.

He waved off her concern.

The duc's father, the Comte d'Artois, and his brother, the Duc d'Angouleme, pushed past them and prostrated themselves beside the dying man. Everyone who was nearby heard de Berri beg to see the king.

The room and hallway were stifling, filled with marshals and ministers of France, bejeweled ladies, and beribboned courtiers standing on tiptoe, mesmerized by the tragedy.

Word had passed down. "The dagger penetrated to the hilt." Dupuytren, the leading doctor among the medical men who had arrived from everywhere, did not pare his prognosis even before his patient. The wound was mortal, he said for all to hear.

He ordered de Berri taken to the manager's office, where they planned to bleed him. Soon de Berri's cries were terrible and mixed with Marie-Caroline's uncontrollable weeping was heartbreaking to hear. André and Nevil insisted that they leave. Turning to go, they heard the duc call out to his wife.

"My dearest, control yourself for the sake of our child."

For many in the dense crowd, it was the first word that the young duchesse was expecting a child.

"If it is a boy, then the assassin has struck for nothing," André whispered to Nevil. "There is still hope for a legitimate heir."

The ride home was accomplished in silence. Too worn out by the night's sad conclusion, the women went immediately to their rooms. André and Nevil changed their clothes and planned to return to the opera house. But first Nevil wrote a report to Tarn Maitland with preliminary word of the tragedy.

While they summoned a fresh carriage, Colby appeared at the door of André's office. She was dressed in a demure gray dress and cloak, pale but stonily composed.

"I am going with you."

"Return to your room, madam," Nevil said harshly.

"If you try to stop me, I shall shout the house down." Colby was not about to be dismissed cavalierly or otherwise. She knew she was seeing history at firsthand, and no one was going to cheat her of it.

Browning looked at his watch. He had no time to argue if he was to get word to Tarn. And knowing his wife, it would avail him nothing to cry a peal over her stubbornness. He gave in, but not gracefully. She was, he confessed, too much of a handful, and he was too tired and depressed to make a scene.

Despite his sorrow, André laughed, and the moment for turning Colby away passed. Thank heaven, Barrault told himself again, French women, even his sister Rita, were more tractable.

The carriage was announced.

They stopped briefly at the British Embassy, woke the ambassador, and informed him of the assassination and left Maitland's letter to be dispatched posthaste to London.

As a witness to the stabbing, Nevil was permitted to sit in on the interrogation of the murderer. Police and government officials tried to bar Colby, but she was ready for them.

"If you turn me away," she said sweetly, "his lordship will not aid you in your inquiries."

Nevil almost choked at her audacity, but he recovered and made great English upper-class noises of the sort that English minions would understand and fall before. Added to Comte André Barrault's consequence, the strange trio were allowed to enter.

The attacker was being held at the Conciergerie near the opera house, where de Berri lingered close to death. Jean-

Pierre Louvel was an unremarkable-looking dark-haired, dark-eyed man bent on murder, who worked as a saddler in the royal stables. At once Browning had his suspicions confirmed. The knife was one commonly used around horses.

Louvel's capture by a food vendor and guards soon after the stabbing was straightforward, and André and Browning were certain his confession was achieved without coercion. Indeed, he seemed happy to repeat his statement over and over to anyone who would listen.

"At least it doesn't seem like a conspiracy," Colby whispered to André and Nevil.

"Too soon to tell," Nevil said quietly and cautioned her to be silent.

She abhorred the man's crime, but seeing and hearing him talk was thrilling. She felt like a voyeur. She knew she should be more decorous, thinking of the duchesse and her child. Indeed, she felt great pity for them, but at the same time she wanted to hear for herself why he hated de Berri enough to kill him.

Louvel said in an even voice that he had been stalking his victim for four years. He had trailed him to theaters where he thought he could find him, during hunts and other public occasions he heard about in the stables. He had even ridden outside the duc's carriage one day. Single-minded in his pursuit, he never made friends or had women in his life.

"I hate the Bourbons, the cause of all of France's problems," he shouted at his questioners.

"And why did you choose the duc?" an official wearing judicial robes hammered at him.

"He was the trunk, the man who personified the hopes of the monarchy," the assassin said. "And if he had escaped, I would have killed his father or his brother."

Neither the assassin nor the questioner dared mention the name of the king as the next in line for murder. A low murmur of distress was heard in the room.

It was an hour before dawn when the trio left and went to the opera house to hear the latest news of de Berri. They walked companionably in the dry, cold night while the carriage followed. Despite the terrible events of the past hours, Colby felt drawn to Nevil as never before. A voice of reason within her warned her against asking for the moon. She had her plans and had sworn to keep them sacred. But reason was not what Colby wanted this night.

"I agree with Colby. I don't think Louvel is an instrument of any party or cabal," Nevil said after a while. "His is a diseased mind, possessed of an idée fixe."

Colby was jubilant. Nevil sided with her!

"The Royalists will not believe your conclusions," André said morosely.

"Will there be blood in the streets tomorrow over this?" Colby asked.

Before he could tell her, they heard carriages and horses in the background, and the king's entourage with a troop of soldiers hove into view near the opera house.

André stood at attention, fighting tears.

"De Berri begged for him hours ago. What took him so long?" Colby was incredulous at the delay.

Nevil turned to her, his eyes glaring. He signaled for the Barrault carriage and rushed her to it. Colby couldn't understand what was happening.

"Take her ladyship home at once," he ordered the coachman.

"You are headstrong and unfeeling and have no right to question a Frenchman or the actions of his king," he said grimly before closing the coach door. "This is not England, and he is not the Regent to be criticized by everyone. You think you may go anywhere and say anything that comes into your head."

He slammed the door and the carriage tore off, leaving Colby speechless with shame. *He is right. I have become incorrigible, wanting my own way all the time. It is unwomanly, but I can't help speaking my mind.*

Encouraged by her father to have opinions, too used to bending her family to her will, she was often impetuous, unthinking, and she knew it. Perhaps this time she had gone too far, and she regretted the way her tongue too often ran away with her. But she did not feel that what she had said was wrong. She only regretted Nevil's anger.

The coach lurched over the uneven cobblestones in the eerie half-light of dawn, and Colby's tears coursed down her face unchecked.

Chapter 29

Paris was draped in mourning, and the Barraults and Brownings moved at funeral pace in their daily lives for more than a week.

The only talk heard anywhere in the capital was of de Berri's death at dawn the morning after the attack and the welcome news that Marie-Caroline was expecting a child in September. The Royalists prayed for a boy to carry on the Bourbon heritage.

Nevil and André and most of the elite went about armed, afraid that rabid Royalists and their sympathizers would lash out at the Bonapartists and Liberals, but there were few demonstrations or incidents of violence. Charges flew far and wide in political circles and the newspapers, however.

Of all of them at the house, Colby was the saddest, not only for Charles and Marie-Caroline, but for what she chose to think was the last chance she and Nevil had of happiness together. She went over in her mind the way he had seemed proud of her insistence on going to the investigation and had actually smiled at her during his interrogation by police officials. She could have built on that had she kept her thoughts to herself. But no, whatever was in her heart was on her tongue, and she had spoiled the moment.

Since that night, Nevil was sure that if he entered a room when she was alone, she got up and left. When he came to her bedroom, she froze before his eyes, and he left in a hurry.

What made matters worse, Colby had become, if possible, more breathtaking as a woman. He yearned to hold her in his arms, to give her the child he felt would complete his life, to tell her things about himself that no one knew. But there was nothing in her manner toward him, no sign that she wanted anything from him except his money and as much distance between them as she could achieve.

It was in this state that they and the Barraults journeyed to Colonel and Mrs. Marrow's home just outside Paris for a private dinner party. Public revelry was frowned on for society, but intimate affairs at home went on.

Like most Parisians, Rita Faberge lived for parties, balls, and operas, the milk of life, and she blossomed at the chance to leave the house and see people.

"I cannot wait to hear Sherrod Marrow's tales tonight," she said gaily as they set out. "He seems to know everything and everyone, that man."

"He's a dear, and Adele is an angel." Colby was laying the groundwork for something she hoped would happen later that evening. Marrow held the key to her future, and she needed to be alone with him.

The Marrows were as eager to see them as the Barrault party was to be out of the gloomy, old mausoleum. Their hosts' mansion was England transported to Paris. Colby wanted to cry. She was so homesick.

Masses of flowers filled the charming house. English landscapes and family portraits everywhere were exactly what Colby needed to feel her spirits revive.

They trooped into dinner and sat at a smaller version of the main dining table. The room was huge and the furniture as English as treacle pudding, and just as homey.

Marrow was immediately besieged with questions. He was delighted to oblige. They were always an eager audience, and he waxed eloquent under their interest.

"What do you want to know?"

"Why was the king so long in coming to see Charles?" Rita wanted to know.

Colby's head reared up, her soup spoon in midair. Nevil choked on his wine. They avoided looking at each other, but watched André. He had been morose for days, blaming himself for not being diligent enough in warning de Berri of the danger.

"Yes. Where was Louis?" André asked.

"He was notified at two o'clock in the morning, but on the advice of Charles's father, he did not go immediately."

"But why?" André demanded.

"Comte d'Artois felt that if the king were present, there would be 'the constraint of etiquette.' Those were his exact words," Marrow reported.

"What does that mean?" Rita wanted to know.

Colby interrupted before Marrow could reply.

"It means, Rita, the poor man would not have been allowed to scream in excruciating pain while those butchers bled him and the king looked on," Colby said bitterly. "In India we did things better."

"It is not your place, madam, to make such comments," Nevil interposed coldly.

"Let us hear what happened next." André was insistent.

"At four o'clock, when all was lost, the king, his gout most troublesome, was hoisted into his carriage and driven in silence to the opera house." Marrow stopped to order his butler to top up their glasses. "It was a great struggle to lift Louis's chair in the narrow precincts, but they did. When Charles saw him, he lifted his head and cried out, 'Forgive me, my uncle, I beg you to forgive me.'"

André and Rita wept openly.

" 'There is no hurry. We will talk about it later,' Louis said. Charles replied, 'Alas, the king does not consent, and yet his forgiveness would have softened my last moments.' And he fell back against his pillows."

Marrow was overcome by his own recital and had to take a breath before continuing.

"Louis looked at the doctors and asked in Latin if there was any hope. They replied it was desperate. The king said, 'Then God's will be done.' A few moments later one of the doctors asked if anyone had a mirror. The king volunteered his snuffbox, and it was held against de Berri's mouth. The doctor pronounced him dead. 'Help me, I have one last service to render.' Holding the surgeon's arm, Louis leaned over and closed Charles's eyes. We all fell on our knees."

Only the hiss of the candle flame was heard when the

colonel finished his story. No one spoke. At last they stood and left the room, each lost in his own world.

Colby succeeded in drawing Marrow into a side room moments before the party broke up. She handed him a note.

"Read it after I leave, and if you will help me, meet me tomorrow at the little park near André's house." She named an early hour and was gone.

Just before they arrived home, André asked Colby what she meant when she said they did things better in India.

"It was stupid to bleed de Berri after he had lost so much blood," she said testily. "Indian doctors use an extract from the leaves of ayapana trees to staunch blood, for heaven's sake!"

"It avails us nothing to speculate," Nevil said bleakly.

"But Charles was attended by the greatest doctors in France," Rita persisted.

Colby shrugged. She was making a nuisance of herself once again to speak her mind so openly. To criticize French doctors would be considered by Nevil another lapse in good taste and further annoy him.

Chapter 30

Colby slept fitfully and woke at dawn, sick at her stomach, barely managing to make it to her dressing room. If I have to go through this for nine months, she told herself, I will go off my head. And I shall have deserved it. Why couldn't I have been sensible and taken Nevil's offer of a loan. But no, I had to be a bloody martyr, and now I am paying for it.

She made her way back and fell heavily onto the bed, waiting for the shaking in her legs to subside. She had hours to wait before she could even think of seeing Sherrod, if he came at all.

At seven, Ilene Merl stole into the room and looked at her mistress stretched across the bed, her nightdress over her knees, her hair curled tight to her head, damp with perspiration.

"My lady, are you unwell?" She flew to the bed.

Colby struggled upright, taking great breaths of air. "Quiet, you'll wake the house," she managed to say between new waves of nausea.

"Are you all right?" the maid whispered.

"I won't die of it, though I may want to in time."

"What are you saying, my lady?"

"Use your loaf, girl," Colby laughed.

The penny dropped, and Ilene raised her hands in praise of heaven and would have shouted in joy if Colby hadn't stopped her in time.

"Quiet. Now lay out my riding costume and go away."

The maid would have argued, but Colby warned her again to be quiet. An hour later, her stomach reasonably in its accustomed place, she dressed, noting with disgust that her waistline was already spreading. She left the house by a back door.

She walked the boundaries of the tiny park for another hour and was about to return to the house when Marrow at last drove up in a smart carriage. Handing the reins to a tiger, he came to meet her.

"I drank a deal too much after you all left, and overslept." His smile was wan and his eyes badly bloodshot.

She hugged him.

"Then you mean to help me?"

"I mean to listen," he said warily.

"Sherrod darling, I'm counting on you to help me leave Paris in the next few days and arrange passage to England for me and my maid."

Marrow suspected that was her plan as soon as he read her note. For a big, blustery ex-soldier who liked to give the impression that he was nothing more than a simple gossip and ranking snob, he was all those things and more. Wily, curious, generous, he was a man to trust when his head and heart were touched. And he liked Colby enormously from the first moment they met.

"I shall do all that, my dear, if you tell me the truth about why you are deserting your husband."

However much she had weighed the reasons for leaving Paris, Colby had never seen her actions as desertion.

"Nevil doesn't love me, and I don't love him," she said, trying not to falter over the harsh words. "It was a marriage made in desperation."

Marrow was startled.

"Has he been cruel to you?" He was miserable at the thought that Nevil was not the gentleman he expected. "I can't accept any son of Monton and Miriam Browning would be a swine to his wife."

"Not in the way you mean," she hurried on. "My job is to produce an heir and get out of his life, and that is precisely what I am proposing to do. I simply don't want to concern him with details. Please help me."

Marrow wished he'd consulted his wife. He knew why he

hadn't. She would have disapproved, calling him an old med-
dler. And she would have been right.

"I still don't see why you want to leave now," he argued.
"You will be returning to England soon enough now that his
job is finished."

Colby disliked stretching the truth, but she wanted to be
away more than she wanted to be honorable.

"He does not feel he has finished that job, and I cannot wait
any longer," she said, pretending tears she was far from feeling. She reckoned wisely that the last thing that a gentleman of
Sherrod's stripe could resist was a woman's tears. She was
half right. He hated tears, but he was determined to be sure of
her motives.

"Why won't he permit you to leave?"

"I haven't asked him," she said. "I don't want to ask him for
anything. I married him for his money, if you must know."

If Sherrod knew anything, he knew Colby Browning was
not a common fortune hunter. A long, successful career in the
army had taught him a good deal about human nature, and it
was this knowledge that led him to the right conclusion about
people most of the time. He waited for her to go on, and seeing
she had no alternative, Colby told him the real story of her
sham marriage, the whole story. In the end she felt better for
someone else knowing about her unhappiness. Confession was
good for the soul, she laughed to herself. Clichés, she decided,
were home truths people could not abide, but still truths.

"If I don't mistake you, Colby, it was a difficult thing for
you to tell me all this."

This time her tears were genuine.

"When do you mean to leave?"

"As soon as I can."

Marrow took out his diary and consulted some dates.

"In three days' time I shall have arranged everything," he
said, replacing the book. "You will have a letter from me giving you all the details."

Colby nodded gratefully. Then the matter of money for her
trip came to mind, and she blushed.

"I must ask you to make the cheapest arrangements for us."

"Surely he doesn't keep you short on rations?"

"He has been very generous, but I haven't the heart to ask for anything more than what I must have for my brothers and my house."

At once, Marrow understood the situation better than anything she had told him so far. His cousin might not love Colby, but all her protestations about her real feelings for Nevil were skewered. She was more than in love with her husband, and for that he envied the man enormously. She was a one-in-a-million woman, and Nevil was a congenital idiot not to know it and cherish her.

Marrow bent forward to kiss her cheek.

"Leave it to me, my dear."

She watched him walk to his carriage and returned to the house.

Chapter 31

For the next two days, Nevil sought the courage to approach Colby and seek peace between them. Her seeming withdrawal from all that went on about her was crushing to him and felt by the Barraults, he was sure.

Nevil's irritation with Colby's tactlessness had long since dissipated. He had to admit that he should not have been so hard on her, but he had been overtired and more upset than he realized at witnessing the assassination and, yes, for not preventing it. Attacking the king in André's hearing was the last straw. It pained him to admit it now, but the truth was that at the time he, too, thought Louis had taken an unconscionably long time to console his nephew.

In a strange way, he told himself, the carnage at Badajoz, which he thought was long behind him, the assassination, and the death of Robert were linked, and the cause of his continued despondency. Violence was becoming more abhorrent to him every day.

He wondered if his desire for a son didn't have something to do with it. And, yes, he finally acknowledged, I want a child of my own. I want one desperately.

At once Nevil could understand why Charles de Berri, tortured by the doctors, hearing his wife's screams mixed with his own, knowing he was dying, pleaded with Marie-Caroline to remember that she carried their child. He wanted to tell all this to Colby, but he was paralyzed by her remoteness, her obvious need to be alone and as far away from him as possible. At meals she sat quiet and unresponsive.

Every attempt to draw her into conversations was met with

politeness, but nothing more. She rarely spoke, just sat haunt-ingly alone and removed. Nevil blamed himself. Why had he felt it necessary to curb her at every turn? He knew from the first that no one could ever control her, and yet he had stupidly persisted. His head was spinning with recriminations, but he kept putting off confessing his errors, waiting for the right mo-ment.

Colby was grateful that dinner the night before her flight was fortunately enlivened by the appearance of the Marrows at André's table. Rita was in rare form, her wit devastating, her stories about her legion of lovers notoriously wicked, but very amusing. Her brother was beginning to take less blame for the tragedy. With Paris relatively calm, he felt able to return to talk of the future.

André smiled indulgently at his guests. He had a surprise for them.

"I think we should all leave Paris for a long weekend," André suggested over dessert. "Snow is thick on the ground, and the chateau is being readied for us."

They were delighted. The assassination had been difficult for them, and a chance to leave it all behind was a godsend.

Colby joined the rest of the table in making plans, never by word or act giving away her secret. She was off at daybreak, and in her reticule was the itinerary Marrow had organized down to the last detail and given to her before dinner earlier in the evening.

"I trust I am doing the right thing in fostering this plan of yours," the colonel had said miserably.

"You see, Nevil has no interest in me, never has," Colby told him, taking his hand. "I will do my duty and present him with an heir, and we shall live as strangers. That is the way we both desire matters should stand."

Privately, Marrow thought his cousin was a fool, but he was too old and mellow to tell him so. If he had seen one sign of affection on Nevil's part, he would have refused to help Colby, even at this late date. But he had seen only cold cor-rectness.

Unlike so many men of his time, Sherrod Marrow did not believe a woman was a chattel to be ordered about, dominated or disregarded at will, no matter what current mores dictated. He had seen too much gratuitous marital cruelty, both physical and mental, in his set in London and France, and was at odds with men who degraded women. He laughed when people spoke of his own wife's easy ways. Actually, she was a delightful tyrant and ruled him and their staff like a tartar.

Marrow sighed. The older he got, the more he realized he knew less about the world and human nature than he thought. For all that he loved doing kind things for people, such as the luxurious plans he made for Colby. His majordomo would accompany her to Calais and see her safely aboard a ship to Dover.

Later, Colby fled to her bedroom long before the party broke up.

"We leave at first light for London tomorrow morning," she told her maid. "Pack only enough to get home."

The girl was appalled to leave so many wonderful clothes behind and would have argued, but Colby's cold voice showed she was determined to have her way.

"Ilene, I do not propose to discuss this," she warned, and the maid retreated. "If you desire to remain here until his lordship returns home, you may do so."

"It will take me an hour to pack, madam," she said, setting to work.

She saw the hurt look on Ilene's face and smiled to reassure her. Colby had to steel herself for the journey. If the truth were told, she wasn't completely sure of the wisdom of her escape and the reasons for it. But it was too late for refining on anything that might weaken her resolve.

"My family needs me," Colby said softly by way of soothing the girl and convincing herself. "I have been away too long."

The maid smiled, relieved that her mistress was no longer upset with her.

The two worked side by side in silence, and the task was accomplished quickly. But the irrepressible Ilene could not help secretly including a few of the fabulous clothes made for Colby by the Parisian dressmakers.

Colby was firm. She would never forgive herself if she took anything more than she absolutely needed. She wanted few reminders of her honeymoon and Nevil's limitless generosity.

They had just completed their labors when they heard Nevil and his valet in the dressing room.

"Go and pack your things, and meet me here at five tomorrow," Colby said, shooing the girl out of the room. "Don't talk to anyone."

Dressed in her nightgown, Colby took her writing desk to bed and hastily wrote two letters, addressed them, and blew out the candle. Too tired and drained to sleep, she lay against the pillows, trying to block out the noises from the other room and the man who made them.

It seemed like an eternity since Nevil had come to her bed, but her yearning for him, far from abating, seemed to grow stronger. Nothing she could say to herself eased the pain and need of him. She relived every moment they had been together like a holy ritual. No matter how hard she tried, she could not block them from her mind. Nevil was like a fever in her body, and the more she raged against his power over her, the more she knew she was powerless to cure herself.

I will never stop fighting him. Everything will change once I regain the sanity of England and Brawleigh. I'll lose myself in work. I will. I must. She closed her eyes, trying to stem the scalding tears that had become the prelude to sleep and oblivion every night.

The door opened, and a shaft of light fell across the bed. She held her breath against the heat that rose up to betray every promise she had made.

With all the will in the world, Colby wasn't sure she had the strength to deny him, even on this last night. She waited. The light faded as quickly as it came. More than anything else, Colby wanted to reach out to him. But it was not in her nature to apologize for something she felt was a horrible injustice. She could see that she might have been more diplomatic, but Nevil knew it was not one of her gifts. Still, she was miserable.

Chapter 32

Brawleigh lay dark and brooding in the night.

August Panaman had been studying the house from every angle for hours, waiting for nightfall.

"The south wind is the place we go to first, understand?"

"I can't do it." Harvey Cortnage's voice was thick with terror.

Panaman swore and extracted a dueling pistol from his pocket. The old muzzle at the back of the neck drove the other down the slope, the unlit torch falling out of his hand. He tripped over it, speeding his descent.

"It's lead or light, you coward bastard," August Panaman warned when he caught up with him. He was enjoying the other's fear and made no secret of it. "I'm finished waiting for the bitch."

The plan was to crouch as low as they could and run across the high grass of the unmowed lawn like bats out of hell.

"I put somethin' in the dogs' pails at nightfall, but you never know," Panaman said. "Don't hang about. They might smell us."

"Jesus, when did you bathe last?" Cortnage hissed, hoping to bolster his courage with the insult. His stomach heaved. The one-time estate manager had gone ever more to seed and appeared more deranged each time he saw him. Cortnage cursed himself for ever getting involved with the man.

On signal, they broke into a run, lighting the torches as they neared the house.

Chapter 33

Rita Faberge hurried into the dining room, her beribboned morning gown flowing behind her. Her brother and the servants didn't know what to make of her. It had been years since any of them had seen her at the breakfast table, and disheveled as well.

"Pierre, go away and take the others with you," Rita told the butler. "And close the door behind you."

André smiled at his sister. Everything in her life was a Racine drama, and he waited for this one to unfold.

"Colby has left Nevil."

It took a great deal to rattle André Barrault.

"Are you saying in your inimitable way that Colby has gone without Nevil's permission?"

"Precisely, you goose. One would need to be blind not to notice the coldness between them, but to run away, fantastic," she said, enjoying her news. "The trouble is that she loves him, but he, the epitome of cold Britishness, is indifferent."

André shrugged. He would have known how to keep Colby happy, but that was neither here nor there. As he pondered the matter, Nevil arrived with Pierre behind him carrying a silver urn of fresh coffee.

He kissed Rita on the cheek.

"You look lovely, as usual," he said and took his place at the table. "This is an unexpected pleasure."

He missed the worried glances brother and sister exchanged, giving his attention to his correspondence stacked beside his place. The first letter, written in a sweeping hand, was not one he knew, but the scent was familiar. He took it up at the same time as he became aware of a lull in the conversation. He looked up and caught his host and hostess trying unsuccessfully to hide some sort of secret.

"Am I de trop?" he asked anxiously, afraid he'd come in the middle of family business.

André and Rita waited until the servants served Nevil.

"Pierre," André said peremptorily. The servants vanished again.

"Colby is on her way to England," Rita said, her eyes shining with excitement. "I think the letter you are holding is from her."

Nevil looked dumbly at the envelope, nodded, and rose from the table. He took the stairs two at a time and arrived in his room seconds later.

The letter was brevity itself.

"I have fulfilled my part in this farce. I am returning home."

Nevil flung the letter across the room and followed it, tearing it into pieces. He walked to the window shouting imprecations he hadn't used since his days as a serving officer.

Nevil's first instinct was to run after Colby and, short of hauling her back by the hair, force her to return to Paris. But his pride wouldn't allow that. If the nights they had shared before the death of the Duc de Berri meant nothing, then he would wipe out every trace of her in his life. She had sinned against him, and he would resume his life without her. That had been their bargain in the first place. Why should he let her know the power she had gained over him?

Nevil returned to the dining room as if nothing had happened. Rita might not like it, but to do otherwise would have been the height of stupidity.

The Barraults watched openmouthed, all urbanity wiped clean. Nevil asked a footman to fix a plate for him as casually as if it were any morning of his life.

Rita had thought him cold. Now he was gelid.

"My wife and I have an understanding," he said with consummate savoir faire. "We lead our lives differently than most people. You French do not own the pattern on civilized marriages, you know."

Nevil looked at Rita, daring her to doubt his word. He underestimated her.

"You talk errant nonsense," Rita said, undaunted.

"Silence!" André was raging. "How dare you interfere."

"Your wife is expecting a child, and some women act strangely at those times." She was out of patience with both of them. "Go after her, you fool, and bring her back like any reasonable husband would."

"Rita, leave this table, or remember your place," André was beside himself.

"You mistake me, madam, if you think that makes a scintilla of difference." Nevil held up his hand to keep André from ordering his sister out of the room. "My wife, as you must be aware, is a very strong-willed woman. We respect our different interests."

André Barrault looked long and hard at his friend and didn't believe a word he said. For once he agreed with his outrageous sister. Once before he had seen Nevil Browning devastated by a woman, and it hadn't been a pretty picture. For all his British sangfroid, André would have bet half his fortune that Browning was anything but indifferent to Colby. But he had never told a man how to deal with his wife, and he was not about to start now.

"When shall we leave for the country?" he asked, effectively putting a period to further discussion.

Chapter 34

Colby stared unseeing at the French countryside racing past the windows of the marvelously sprung carriage Colonel Marrow had put at her disposal.

The long journey from Paris had been as comfortable and speedy as he and the man he had designated as courier could contrive. She and Ilene had stayed at picturesque inns and guest houses, where the name Marrow assured them a glorious welcome and the warmest of feather beds. The array of French cuisine that was presented to her could more than stand comparison with any of the viands she had been served in Paris.

Then why am I not happy, thrilled, in fact, to be nearing England? Wasn't that what I wanted from the beginning, to be rid of Nevil and reunited with the family?

"My lady, are you feeling unwell?" The maid was appalled at the misery that appeared on her mistress's face too often these past days to suit her. "Shall I ask Monsieur Joseph to stop awhile?"

"Absolutely not!" Colby said impatiently. "You know I want to be at home as soon as may be."

Ilene's country wits told her differently, but it was not her place to question the evidence of her own eyes, and she kept her tongue between her teeth. She was not so easily deluded, and she had, since leaving Paris, seen her mistress dawdle too often over the most trivial things, as if waiting for something. Or was it someone? A tall, blond man as handsome as a picture, a man no reasonable woman would throw out of her bed or leave to the mercy of those painted Frenchwomen, if

Comtesse Faberge was an example of the breed. Ilene hadn't seen much of the master as she would have liked, but she had a ready, bawdy imagination, and that was enough for her to have dreams far above her station.

Perhaps she was being romantic, but she had trembled with excitement, expecting her master to find them and bring them back to Paris. Maybe London paragons were different, but no countryman of her experience would have permitted his wife to go haring away without his authority. And the urgency and secrecy of their departure had all the earmarks of an escape, and no one could tell her otherwise. The gentry were not always easy to understand, and her head ached with thinking about things that were beyond her ken.

After making sure that Colby was comfortable, she feigned sleep, the better to imagine Nevil Browning with his boots beneath her bed.

The sight of the tall ships lying at anchor in the teeming port of Calais was far from consoling, as Colby had envisioned when she had made her plans. She had never given a thought to the crossing to Dover, twenty-five miles across the Channel in the small ship that awaited them the next morning. Never much of a sailor, the boats bobbing like so many corks, caused her stomach to lurch alarmingly.

Monsieur Joseph was kindness itself and insisted that she rest in the carriage while he organized her baggage and saw to the stateroom that had been booked for her.

She watched the little Frenchman start for the boat and talk briefly with an officer at the foot of the gangway. He returned, his brows knitted in concern. He was the father of ten children and much experienced with pregnant women. The pinched and greenish color that had overtaken his lovely charge was not to his liking. Colonel Marrow would not be at all pleased if he did not continue to do his best for his friend.

"Perhaps we should wait another day when the water will be calmer? They are expecting a storm."

Colby was within an ace of falling in with his suggestion, but she wanted to put as much distance as she could between

herself and her husband. Not that there was much hope that
Nevil planned to bestir himself to prevent her from leaving.

Much against her wishes, the route from Paris mapped out
by Colonel Marrow and Monsieur Joseph had left a trail a
blind man could have followed, she told herself bitterly. But
Nevil had not followed them, and she was forced to believe
that her absence suited him too much. It was a lowering
thought, but what else had she expected? Colby knew she was
being unreasonable, and that was even less comforting.

"The gentleman is right," Ilene seconded from her seat in
the corner of the carriage. She, too, had chosen not to think
about the miserable crossing on Browning's luxurious yacht.
The boat in the harbor appeared about as sturdy as a punt, and
she prayed that the indecision she saw in Colby's face would
prevail. What would one more day on dry land hurt? No one
was chasing them, unfortunately.

"I cannot wait another day," Colby managed to say as a
spasm of nausea attacked her.

"As Madame wishes," Monsieur Joseph replied and left
them to complete his arrangements.

Once aboard, Colby fell on the bunk fully clothed, barely
able to determine what the courier was trying to tell her.

"The first mate has been instructed to procure a suitable
coach in Dover for the last part of your journey," he said,
but he wasn't sure she was attending. His good soul made
him go beyond the colonel's instructions. "You are not at all
comfortable. If you desire it, I can take you to your destination."

Much as she liked the man's company, and indeed had
wondered how she and Ilene would have fared on their own,
Colby had no other wish than to be left alone and miserable in
peace. She recalled all his courtesies to her and her maid, and
rose from the bed to give him her hand and a large donation
for his hopeful family. They parted with excessive compliments.

When the door closed, Colby found a pail and was miserably sick. She hated everything about illness in herself. She
was a good nurse, but a bear with a sore head when anything
befell her.

Once again the thought that she had months of this facing her did nothing to lighten the heaviness that had become all too familiar since she met Browning.

Ilene arrived cheery and excited with a spring in her step that made Colby groan.

"I met the handsomest officer, madam, and he said he will take us in charge when we arrive in England," she chirped merrily as she set about arranging Colby's nightclothes.

"I don't mean to be sick on this trip, madam," she said confidently.

Colby didn't want to be churlish, and if Ilene magically acquired a secret remedy between shore and the half hour they were aboard, she hoped she would share it.

"Men have no liking for vomit," Ilene went on wisely.

Some men don't care, Colby amended silently. The last thing she wanted to think about was the exceptional man who had performed heroically, even if she had slept through most of his ministrations. Sometimes it didn't do to remember too much.

"Would you mind, my lady, if I took a turn on the deck and watched the boat leave harbor?"

Cupid had made greater strides than Colby could have predicted, and she was only too glad to promote young love if it meant she could suffer in private. Normally she delighted in Ilene's good sense and inconsequential chatter, but not today. She waved the girl off and turned her face to the wall.

The storm hit in the early hours, awakening Colby from a troubled sleep. She couldn't remember where she was until her eyes picked out a faint light in the cabin near where Ilene lay snoring in a corner chair.

The ship was defying the laws of gravity, making the most intricate geometric patterns known to man and the devil. Monsieur Joseph had been right, of course. She should have waited for another day. But when did she ever not go her own way? The last voice she heard was always her own, whatever the consequences. One day, Colby told herself, I will learn to take advice. But she doubted it.

In spite of feeling like something that lived in a sty, she found that she could smile. Indeed, the ridiculousness of her situation sent her into a fit of laughter. She had run away from one of the most palatial houses in all of Paris, surrounded by the last word in luxury, only to catapult herself into the middle of the Strait of Dover in what was probably a gale, and assuredly in a bathtub of a boat.

To add to the absurdity, she was clammy and hot and chilled at the same time. The traveling costume she had worn the day before smelled to high heaven, yet she felt better than she had in months. This time she let out a wicked cackle and threw her legs over the side.

In some miraculous way, which she thought wiser not to examine too closely, she felt amazingly alive, excited, and optimistic all at once. She was on her way home, she had a thousand tales to tell the boys and Aunt Sylvia, and she was about to make Brawleigh a showplace with all the money she could need.

Besides, she was bored with feeling fragile. Since her father died she had no one to lean on and over the past weeks had given in too easily to the wishes and needs of others. I'm free she cried out and threw off all the chains that had bound her.

"You are awake at last," Ilene called out.

"Yes, and I am going on deck."

The maid couldn't believe it. Lady Colby, in her short experience of her, had never sounded so ready for a lark. She stood up, and the boat took a leap, sending her crashing against the wall. Colby braced her legs against the bunk and more than ever was determined to leave the cabin. She had to see for herself what was happening outside.

"Where have you put my clothes?"

"You can't leave the cabin."

"I'm going!"

"I can't find my feet, much less your clothes," the maid wailed. Her ladyship wasn't moving off the chair where the last rolling motion had deposited her.

"Nonsense," Colby shouted above the roaring in the timbers. "Point me to them, and take my bed. I won't need it again."

One could not live in the country where there was a legend for everything, Ilene thought, and not hear all the stories about the strange ways some women behaved when they were increasing. Only that could explain Lady Colby's sudden change of mood.

"Can a servant forbid her mistress to do something that may harm her?" Ilene asked plaintively.

"You goose." Colby helped her to the bunk.

Colby washed her face and hands and hastily changed her clothes, wrapping herself in a huge, gray cloak that Rita Faberge's dressmaker had made for her. Fortunately, Ilene had refused to leave it behind.

Dawn was just breaking and bathed the angry waters in a silvery light.

"You are a hearty soul, Lady Browning."

Colby turned to see the captain and first officer pause in their examination of the damage caused by the vile weather.

"Thank you. I consider that a compliment." Colby gave them a smile, pleased beyond anything that they received her with grave admiration.

"A cup of tea with some fortifying rum would be in order," the captain offered. "Will you take it in my cabin, or here?"

"Here, please."

The men saluted and returned to the bridge.

Studying the strait made her think of her first channel crossing. Nevil had told her the deck was the only place to be during a bad time. She had wanted to throw something at him then, and ten times since, but no longer. She tried to fight it, but thinking about Nevil brought back images that threatened her hard-won faith and excitement for the future, a future that would never include the feel of his magnificent body molded against hers, of knowing, tapering fingers that could make her senses come alive and beg for more. He played on her womanhood like a virtuoso.

Damn him, damn him, she screamed into the wind, bringing

her arms about her body and the child growing within, a constant reminder for all her days of the nights she had fought against a frenzied hunger that only Nevil knew how to feed and only he could satisfy.

Chapter 35

Nevil slipped his arm around Rita Faberge's waist as they waltzed in the frigid night, oblivious to the cold. Music spilled over the snow-covered terrace of the Barrault's chateau, bathing them in candlelight from the ballroom beyond.

What had started as a dutiful exercise to please Rita's whim soon became something more. He drew her closer, and she came catlike into him, arching her body, her legs provocatively fitting between his. She felt him harden, and a purr rumbled deep in her throat.

"Nevil . . ."

"Don't spoil it," he whispered hoarsely, his face buried in masses of hair, his warm breath teasing her throat.

They whirled as one, wild abandon and need igniting like a forest fire between them. Rita threw back her head, looked up at him, and approved what she saw. She was winning her siege, and nothing in God's green earth would keep Nevil from falling to her now.

When the music stopped, Rita took his hand, leading him down the length of the terrace to the door of the picture gallery.

André Barrault noticed their long absence, left his guests, and came out of the ballroom just as Rita opened the door. A glint of light on the glass panes drew him toward the gallery.

He could read his sister like a book. It wasn't the first time she had set her cap for Browning. Once her lust was rampant there was no stopping her. No man was safe.

"Rita," he called out, quickening his step. How many times

do I have to rescue her from herself? She has the morals of a rabbit. Not that I am much better, he conceded, but this time he would not let her break her heart over a man who mourned for another.

"My dear, you are neglecting your duties," he said sweetly when he came up to them.

Rita could have strangled him. She knew exactly what André was trying to do. He was becoming a bore, always interfering in her conquests. Nevil was different from most of the men she coveted. He was hers, had been from the moment she first saw him in England when she was a young girl.

Nevil watched the play of temper between sister and brother. He had never seen them quite this disturbed with each other, but didn't intercede. They had always fought like tigers, and it was always over quickly. But he hated to be the cause of their latest battle of wills.

Bedding Rita, desirable as she was, would have been delightful and temporary. He needed to obliterate Colby from his soul, but it was wrong to use Rita or any woman so casually for something impossible.

Now that his ardor had vanished, he was glad that his friend had prevented him from making the biggest blunder of his life. No woman could assuage his need for Colby, which seemed to grow with each hour. *How did I ever give a woman the license to turn me into a figure of derision in my own eyes?* Much as he had tried to deny it, he was suffering like any callow youth. Unrequited love. What a bad joke! The truth had been staring him in the face for weeks. There was no other way to put a good face on it. It was something that happened to dolts, men he'd always pitied, but here he was as moonstruck as the best of them . . . for the second time, too.

"Nevil, tell André to go away," Rita cried, pulling at his sleeve to get his attention.

He had been so absorbed in his own concerns that he hadn't noticed that the two were waiting for him.

"Let's rejoin your guests, my dear," Nevil said, taking her arm.

Rita turned to him.

"No wonder your wife ran away," she spat out and ran back to the ballroom.

Chapter 36

The hired coach had been going at racketing speed when it suddenly veered crazily on a verge on the outskirts of Moreton.

"What now, for heaven's sake?" Colby called out. Her impatience to be home was making her a martinet, but before she could call the coachman to account, she heard a sound that was more beautiful than music. A flock of bleating sheep were strung across the road on their way to market. After an exchange of colorful, original oaths between the shepherd and the coachman that rivaled anything Colby had heard during her years among soldiers, the coach moved at a walk.

"It's good to be home, isn't it, my lady?" Ilene said, half in and out of the window. A Celt to her fingertips, the maid had found foreign travel not at all to her liking. The clean country air was just what they both needed, and the strains and stains of travel fell away.

Colby set aside the carriage rug that Ilene had insisted she wear over her shoulders. Catching the girl's delight, she hung out the window trying to see the town in the distance. To hell with decorum. I am richer than I ever dared think, and I can afford to behave even more outrageously than I have before. Moreton citizenry would expect it of me, she decided, merry and philosophical.

Eccentricity was an endearing quality among her fellow Britons, and with the wherewithal to be indulgent, she intended to enjoy herself from that time onward. Within reason, of course. That was her better self talking. A great deal of social fence mending was in order. Mark and Matthew needed to gain acceptance and entry into polite society at once. They needed boys of their own age. Isolated as they had been because of their uncles' sordid reputations, they had a great deal of catching up to do.

They were fine-looking boys and had charm and sweetness aplenty. Their manners were impeccable; she had seen to that. What they needed most were the very best crammers to make up any gaps in their education. Only Eton, Oxford, or Cambridge would do for those two scamps. Her father would have been pleased. He had given them into her care, and she meant to protect them always.

If her child was a boy, and she fervently hoped it would be, she would not have to scheme and fight as hard as a navvy. Her son would have everything that the Browning name and lineage promised with his first breath of life.

She smiled protectively and folded her hands over her slightly rounded belly. The idea of you, Colby said to herself, may have come of my desperation and your father's grief, but you shall have all the love I am capable of giving. She sat back as contented as she had ever been. If only I can find a faraway place for your father in my mind and my dreams. It will be the hardest task of all, but she would exorcise Nevil Browning from her life. It was a promise. Anything less would be ruinous.

Colby returned to peer out the window, anxious to see if anything could possibly have changed in what seemed an eternity since she was last in the town. The Norman church lay gray and stalwart in the distance, the corn exchange and the building that housed the assembly rooms and lord mayor's office still flanked the town center. The pretty cottages with their small patches of garden passed on each side of them. She was almost home.

Colby waved at a few townspeople, but none returned her greeting. The least fanciful of women, she felt a forbidding strangeness in the way they looked at her and turned to hide their faces. Hadn't they yet forgiven her for ridding them of that animal Panaman? I should have been awarded a medal, not shunned.

"Bastards," she muttered. "Spoiling my homecoming."

The maid couldn't imagine what was perturbing her mistress. It had been a treat to watch Lady Colby change into a lighthearted companion since the night of the storm.

Colby called out. "Give the horses their heads; we've dallied enough."

The coachman obliged, and they were off and running as fast as she could have wished. In half an hour they reached the brow of the hill that overlooked the graystone house a quarter of a mile in the early mist. She couldn't wait to see the perfect symmetry of Brawleigh that always dazzled her whenever she came near.

"Sound your horn, driver," Colby shouted, hanging out the window.

At once she saw that something was wrong, terribly wrong. The outline of the west wing, which had been converted to living quarters to save fuel and work for the greatly reduced staff, was blackened, windows and masonry outlined in the mist at grotesque angles. She looked wildly for signs of life, but nothing and no one appeared.

"Stop the coach," she screamed, opening the door before it could stop and the steps let down. She fell heavily to the ground, unable to control her panic, needing to see things for herself.

She pounded down the driveway, deaf to everything but a terrible fear of disaster, cursing herself for luxuriating in Paris, abandoning them when she should have been at home doing what she did best, protecting them.

Her lungs filled to bursting, tears running down her face, Colby tried to rouse the household, but no one answered. At last the door opened slowly. Her aunt, haggard, a wraith, looking years older, stood with Mark, wide-eyed and frightened, cringing by her skirts.

Colby flung herself forward and gathered them into her arms, hysterical with relief. She looked around, expecting to see Matthew standing behind them.

"Where's Matt?"

"He's alive," Sylvia Rainwriter whispered.

"He's bad, Colly," Mark said. "The pain makes him cry."

He reached for her hand and dragged her to the drawing

room, where Matthew lay huddled on a filthy couch, hollow-eyed, manfully holding back his sobs, his right leg mangled and festering, his hands blackened. She clenched her fists to keep from crying out. She had to be strong for him, for all of them.

"Colly's here," she said, cushioning his head against her breast, her heart sore with pity. "Everything will go better, I promise, darling, and you know I always keep my promises."

Ilene Merl hovered in the doorway, sickened by the putrid odor in the room, afraid for her mistress.

"My lady, can I help?"

"Yes, please," Colby replied, trying for a degree of normalcy. "Get the bag with the gifts, and take my reticule and pay off the driver.

Ilene ran out to the coach.

"Now let's set things to rights," Colby said, mastering her horror, desperately trying to give them her courage. She took off her coat and rolled up her sleeves, her mind racing ahead.

"Aunt Sylvia, please see to some food for us. We're starved." Food was the last thing Colby wanted, but she had to get the household moving until she could decide what needed to be done.

Ilene returned with bags full of presents and set about opening them. The mistress had bought out the shops, but not even a fan for herself.

Colby moved to open the windows, needing fresh air to counter her nausea. This was hardly the time to indulge herself in any way. The deplorable state of her brother's legs and hands, the foulness of the room, its awful disarray told her that events had swamped Sylvia, and she must take charge of their lives once more. The thought was a tonic, and she moved with a renewed vigor.

She went in search of her aunt and found her in the kitchens ordering a scratch meal. Before her wedding, Colby had given her money and instructions to hire several gardeners, maids, and an undercook while she was away. But Sylvia hadn't done a thing.

If she didn't laugh, she would cry, and she was past crying. The injuries to Matthew and the destruction of the west wing had seen to that. She would start at once getting things sorted out. Only she could manage.

Home at last. Everything and nothing had changed, but at least she had the means to improve their lives, won at great cost to her soul, to be sure. She felt better. She knew where she was going.

Colby accepted her staff's congratulations, promised them a celebration as soon as she saw to Matthew's injuries and steered her aunt away to the morning room.

"When was the doctor here last?"

"Several days ago."

"No wonder the boy is suffering," Colby yelled. "Send for him at once."

Sylvia's face crumbled. "He wants to amputate Matthew's leg."

"I won't let that happen." Colby couldn't believe what she heard.

"He said he couldn't speak for the consequences, and I sent word to you, unaware you were on your way home. We haven't seen him since."

For the first time in her life, Colby's nerve began to fail, bewildered as she had never been. She had faced the death of her father and the loss of Brawleigh with unshakable faith that she would somehow prevail. But to hold her brother's life in her hands was devastating. She needed time to think. She needed help, but she had no one to turn to, and the enormity of what had been thrust upon her was crushing.

"What are you going to do?" Sylvia asked, in full assurance that Colby would rescue Matthew. Hadn't she always taken care of them?

Colby was looking blankly out at the neglected, overgrown herb garden outside the room.

"You're not listening." Her aunt stood before her, pulling on her arm.

"I must speak to the doctor," she said. "Send someone for him at once." It was a feeble reply, but she couldn't look at her aunt's face, so hopeful, so certain Colby had the answer.

Sylvia went at once, glad of the chance to be doing something. All will be well when Colby comes home, that was what

she had told the boys in the week since the fire, and she was
well rewarded, as she knew she'd be.

In the time it took for the doctor to appear, Colby had set
everyone to tasks. The drawing room was cleaned and aired,
and between them she and Ilene had managed to bathe
Matthew, cut his hair, change his linens, and straightened the
couch on which he lay. They moved him as little as necessary
and with the gentlest of hands made him as comfortable as
they could.

The boy's fortitude was enormous. His gratitude in having
Colby at his side and the faith he held in her ability to make
him well only added to her burdens.

The doctor arrived just as they finished. Dr. Richard Reed
was fat and hulking, and despite a mane of white hair, of
which he was clearly proud, he was one of the least prepos-
sessing men she had ever met. Colby remembered from her father's final days that Reed's fingernails were often filthy as he
moved in an aura of cheap brandy and stale tobacco. He was
not made to inspire confidence, but he was the best that Moreton had on offer. As chatelaine of Moreton House, all that
would change, Colby told herself.

Colby and Ilene held Matthew still while the doctor cleaned
and bandaged his wounds. The man had the hands but none of
the skills of a carpenter, he was anything but a healer, and if
she could, Colby would have barred him from the house.
Matthew moaned pitifully, and she had to close her eyes to
keep from fainting at his rough treatment of the boy.

What hurt most was the unfairness. Matthew didn't deserve
to suffer when he'd saved the household and by great presence
of mind had prevented Brawleigh from burning to the ground.

When he finished, the doctor gave the boy laudanum and
bade Colby to join him in the hall. But first he looked lovingly
at the brandy bottle on a side table. She poured him a drink,
and together they walked to the door.

"I cannot urge you too strongly, Lady Browning," he said in
his pompous way. "The limb must come off. The leg was
badly broken and burned when he tried putting out the fire
himself and will never be a mite of good to him."

"How much time before I must make that decision?" Colby held her breath.

"I told your aunt it should have been done before this," he said self-importantly. He wasn't used to having his word questioned by any woman.

"How much time do I have before I give my approval?" she pressed for an answer.

"Soon." He drained the glass and left.

Her aunt joined her at the door.

"Ilene tells me you are expecting a child."

Her niece smiled and touched her stomach.

"Does Nevil know?"

"Yes. I left him a note."

"And he didn't stop you?"

Colby nodded and left her standing on the doorstep. It wouldn't do for anyone to see her struggle against the tears that threatened every time she thought about her husband. No one must know how much she regretted her precipitous flight. It was a confession damaging to her peace, for when she had told Ilene that her family needed her, she had no way of knowing how prescient she was.

Stop thinking about him. Stop. You and Nevil were doomed from the start. It is always wrong to ask for the moon.

Colby lay awake on a makeshift bed in the drawing room to be close to Matthew if he needed her in the night. Light from a small candle shadowed the room. He was fretful, and she feared he was more feverish than before. She got up and stood over him, willing him to fight for his life as hard as he had fought the fire.

The thought of having to be the one to decide whether he was to be a cripple all his life haunted her from the moment her aunt told her that was what Dr. Reed wanted to do. How can anyone be forced to have the yea or nay of anything so shattering? What if she said yes, and Matthew never forgave her? What if she said no, and Matthew died? They weren't choices; they were unmitigated catastrophes. God only knew she wasn't Solomon.

"Colby, am I dreaming? Are you really here?"

She jumped up and went to him.

"What is it, darling?" She took up a clean cloth and wet it, passing it gently over his parched lips.

"I have something to tell you." Speech was difficult, and his words came out inaudibly.

"The night of the fire I heard footsteps running toward the house, but I didn't pay attention because the dogs weren't barking." Tears ran down his face. "It was all my fault."

"You did splendidly, Matt." So it *was* arson! It didn't surprise her. Indeed, from the moment she first saw the ravages of the fire, it came to her that it might be the work of Panaman.

Hadn't her aunt told her when she returned from London that witnesses had heard Panaman swear to harm her after she had horsewhipped him? Of course, I didn't pay attention. Why do I think I'm invincible? Why did I have to take it into my head to be the judge and jury and rid the district of that evil man? She had no answers, but all her instincts told her she was right, and that was enough for her.

Sylvia Rainwriter sat up in bed writing furiously. She knew she was inviting trouble. She had seen too much of Colby's determination to have her own way and normally would never consider interfering, but her dear girl was pregnant, and she feared for mother and baby. She knew herself to be a terrible moral coward afraid of confrontations, but this was one time that she needed to be strong.

Chapter 37

Browning stood at the rail as his yacht entered the harbor at Dover, his restlessness to be in London was like a troublesome burr giving him no peace. His departure from Merlieu, the Barraults' chateau, had been accomplished stealthily the morning after André had been his guardian angel and kept him from Rita's bed. He hadn't stopped to look back. He had faced the enemy with fewer qualms than the thought of seeing the French hellcat again. His mind didn't want to deal with Rita Faberge's parting shot to him, but it was useless. Was it possible, as Rita had said, that his coldness drove Colby away? Could she ever have any feelings for him? You haven't a hope. Better to fight the demon hunger that needed Colby more and more night and day. She's lost to you. An icy shiver ran down his spine.

At last the ship made port, and Nevil could turn his mind to other pursuits. He was looking frantically for John Lear to be waiting for him. The secretary had known for weeks when he planned to be home.

The last person he wanted to meet was Cortnage, who, without trying, managed to irritate him more each year in every way. It was his own laziness, his fear of change that made him keep the man around.

"My lord, welcome home," Cortnage managed to say, trying to still his racing heart.

"Where is Lear?" Browning's tone was curt, and he brushed past the man without ceremony. The thought of Cortnage's company back to London was making Nevil furious.

"I have no idea, sir," he said, leading the way with small

mincing steps toward the light traveling coach waiting for them nearby. His groom stood by with one of Nevil's favorite riding horses and a wagon for luggage. "I received a message from one of Captain Maitland's lieutenants telling me to meet you."

"Very well," Browning replied, not overly pleased.

"I was myself on the way to see the state of Moreton House and Brawleigh Hall when the summons came, my lord."

Nevil was overjoyed and seized on the chance to be rid of him.

"Do that. I shall want to know how things stand at both estates."

Cortnage couldn't believe his luck. His portmanteau was packed and full of money. He needed to see Panaman at once.

Colby was awake before anyone in the household, impatient for enough light to assess the damage to the house. If she found any evidence that Matthew was right about someone setting the fire, she would move heaven and earth to stop Panaman once and for all time.

Sylvia Rainwriter found her, covered with soot, her gown torn, her hands bleeding, crawling around the west wing.

"What ever are you digging for?" The older woman was worried. Colby's eyes were heavy from lack of sleep, her face drawn from want of rest as she dug among the ruins for all she was worth.

"Look at these," her niece said, brandishing three torches she'd found in the rubble.

"Someone set the fires, and Matthew heard them."

"He never told me!"

"I am certain as death that it was set by Panaman and someone else, and I am off to town to see the justice of the peace," Colby threw out over her shoulder, running toward the house.

An hour later Colby was dressed in the only riding costume she had taken home from Paris. She wanted to look as rich as the Browning name and prestige could convey.

"Colby, you must remember you are carrying a baby," Sylvia cautioned, knowing it was probably useless. "If you must go to Sir Adrian's, at least take a carriage and one of the men as escort. The conventions must be observed."

"Bother all that," Colby said. As a concession she rode sidesaddle, agreed to have a stablehand pressed into service as a groom, and tore off on Midnight at full gallop, leaving the boy hanging on for dear life in pursuit.

Twenty minutes later, Sir Adrian Moore, the man who passed for keeper of law and order, seated Colby with great ceremony and asked her to join in taking coffee. She smiled and accepted his invitation, fighting down a sharp desire to tell the doddering old man what she really thought of him. He was one of the leaders of society that determined who was and who was not accepted. When she thought how hard and slavishly her mother had fought, unsuccessfully, of course, to be accepted by him and his coterie of blue bloods, she was hard put to keep from throwing the coffeepot at him. Colby marveled at her own forbearance. Blast the need for caution. At any other time she would have given him a setdown he would never forget.

"Allow me to wish you happiness at your wonderful marriage, my dear Lady Colby," he gushed. "I trust you will not keep yourself distant from us now that you reign over Moreton House?"

"I have every intention of making Moreton and Brawleigh the center for anything society can desire," she replied, trying not to choke on her hypocrisy, "but I'm afraid, Sir Adrian, I am here on a most urgent matter, and time is short."

He was all concern and promised his assistance unconditionally.

My word, Colby told herself bitterly. The Browning name can make even this old gelding forget my reprobate uncles and all the other crimes that the Mannering family were damned for until now.

"I am convinced beyond a shadow of a doubt that Augustus Panaman set fire to my house," she said, uncovering the torches she'd brought with her as evidence. She looked at Sir Adrian, waiting for him to examine them.

"I am quite sure you must be mistaken, my dear lady," he said, scowling at the idea she wanted him to soil his hands. "A most unfortunate man to be sure, but no one in his right mind would dare to do anything so deplorable."

Colby waved the torches under his long, aristocratic nose, and he quickly backed away. She tried once again to be pleasant, much as she wanted to rub his face with what she considered incontrovertible proof.

"You are so right, sir," she said, as reasonably as her temper would permit. "The man is mad and bound to destroy me and mine."

"Taking a whip to a proud man before a score of inferiors is not cause to burn down a house as venerable as Brawleigh," Moore observed smugly.

Colby could see that he was certain in his own mind that he was correct. He was so used to being the final authority that he could not allow any conclusion other than his own.

"If he'd been a decent sort, he would not have been the despoiler he was," she reminded him.

"Have you considered that your brothers were playing a lark on your poor aunt and were careless while you were away, shall we say?"

Colby turned the most enraged violet eyes on him.

"You underestimate me, Sir Adrian, if you think I had not made certain that my brothers or anyone else was the cause of the fire," she said, brandishing the torches and parting with words calculated to reduce the old fraud and snob to a blithering idiot. "Shame on you. My husband shall know of your deliberate obstruction."

Colby made her exit slowly enough to allow the man to catch up with her.

"I think you are being too harsh, my lady." His ill-fitting false teeth clicked like a host of beetles. "Let me think again and make some inquiries."

"I dislike having my intelligence called in question, and I no longer have faith in your objectivity. You force me to deal with Panaman in my own way."

Colby remounted and made her way to town. There she promised untold riches and lit up the drab lives of a builder and decorator, who saw guinea signs in front of their eyes when she finished with them.

Brawleigh would live again.

But it was not only pride of place that made her spend Nevil's money, but the assurance that an army of men working about the place for months would give them a measure of protection she was convinced they needed against Panaman. She had no intention of underestimating the fiend.

Later she visited the vicar and made known her needs for additional staff and gave a sizable donation to the church. She planned to stop at Moreton House for a brief meeting with the man who had been Panaman's deputy estate manager. She felt compelled to oversee Nevil's estate, and nothing would keep her from doing it. Moreton, for all its richness, would never be anything more than Nevil's home and her baby's inheritance. She could never imagine living there.

At the point where she needed to turn off the road, a sense of profound weariness overtook her, and she heard again her aunt's cautions. The needs of the child she carried must not be sacrificed, Sylvia had said, and Colby reluctantly turned Midnight homeward. Moreton would have to wait until tomorrow.

She came home laden with news and more gifts, and she let them fuss over her. Matthew smiled wanly, with sunken eyes in a pinched face. He looked no whit better, and she sat beside him trying to will her strength into his scarred body.

"I gave the doctor an earful," Ilene confided to her in a whisper when Colby sent her aunt and Mark into dinner.

"He arrived half foxed, and I told him he was a disgrace."

Colby hugged her. "Was he gentle?"

"Not very, so I gave him a drink and offered to do the bandages," the maid added proudly, "and even if it's me who says it, I was almost as good a nurse as you, my lady."

"You are an angel," Colby said, moved by Ilene's goodness. "When the house is asleep, I will ask you to help me search my father's papers. I think there may be some Indian remedies that could help Matthew."

Later she and Ilene laid waste to the attics. After two hours Colby found a large diary in which she had seen her father make entries from time to time. Under a heading marked "Native Remedies," she saw something about burns. It was written in her father's largely unreadable script, but she could make out that a thick, sticky ointment from the resin of the gum tree was sometimes used to treat powder burns.

"Gum trees can't be plentiful here," she said, discouraged to think how close she might have come to finding something that might give her brother some relief.

Ilene watched her mistress's face glow and then become cast down.

"Tomorrow, when I go to Moreton, I shall consult the head gardener. Perhaps he can help me." Colby rose heavily from the floor. She felt a terrible stabbing pain in her back, and would have fallen if Ilene hadn't caught her.

"My lady, you do too much. Think of the baby," Ilene scolded.

Her conscience hurt as much as the pain. Had she the right to jeopardize her child to her overweening need to be all things to all people? Why was life so hard, forcing her to make Hobson's choices at every turn? She shook her head and was glad to find her way to her bed with her maid's help.

Chapter 38

On her first visit to Moreton the next day, Colby sought out the head gardener, a man whose fame was spread across two counties. He was a grizzled old man, whose family had served the Brownings for over a hundred years, and he was only too happy to put himself at Colby's service. She explained the entry in her father's diary, and he was all attention.

"The resin you describe also comes from the sap of plum peach and cherry trees, my lady, and I have some of those," he told her. He was overcome by her gratitude, and together they went to test her father's notations. They gathered resin samples, and she rushed back to Brawleigh to make an ointment.

On her second visit to Moreton, Colby concluded that it was everything that she wished for Brawleigh. The farms were efficiently run and bountiful, the house grand and welcoming, and for all its size, the family quarters were intimate and homey.

"Panaman may have been the devil incarnate, but he knew what he was about, and the estate shows it," Tommy Evans, the young and vigorous assistant estate manager was telling her as they headed for the main house after an extensive visit to the tenant cottages.

She had been moved to tears by the welcome she was given by the estate workmen and their families. Sir Adrian might think Panaman was incapable of arson, but Nevil's people, victims for years, thought Panaman a monster. They were delighted to see the back of him and told her plainly that she was a heroine for driving him off.

Evans mentioned several times how much he regretted not

having been summoned to help fight the fire at Brawleigh, and this gave Colby an idea.

"Tell me, Evans, would it surprise you if I said I was convinced that Panaman set fire to Brawleigh?" Colby watched the man closely.

"Some of us were wondering about that down at the Anvil, my lady," he replied cautiously. "In for a penny, in for a pound, Lady Browning. But I am sure that many things are missing from the estate."

"What kind of things?" Colby held her breath.

"Tar, guns, ammunition, food stores, and the like."

Colby's ears perked up. "Does anyone know where he went after Lord Browning sacked him?"

"No one has seen hide nor hair of him, and if Augustus doesn't want to be found, he won't be," Evans said emphatically. "He is a famous hunter and knows the country hereabouts like the back of his hand. He has often gone to ground and lived rough. Testing himself, you might say."

Colby brought Midnight to a crunching halt.

"Is anyone here his equal?" Colby asked over the racket Midnight was making circling Evans and his mount.

"There's Shad Pierce, who thinks he's the better man," Evans said, chortling, "and he hates Augustus's guts, if you'll pardon me, Lady Browning. But then, he hates most people."

Colby gave Midnight his head, thinking over what Evans was saying.

"Bring him to me after dark tonight," she said excitedly. "Careful you don't bring attention to yourselves. There'll be something for both of you if we can set the law on Panaman."

Evans and Colby discussed details and rode back toward Moreton House in complete understanding. Colby felt a great burden lifting off her shoulders. She wasn't quite as alone as she'd been.

Colby's high good humor lasted a short time. A splendid traveling coach with its familiar coat of arms stood before the front door, dislodging Lady Miriam Browning and John Lear.

She frowned. Much as she had grown fond of her mother-in-law and Nevil's secretary, she did not want anyone interfering in her life.

She approached them with a false smile masking her extreme irritation.

"My darling girl." Lady Browning gathered her into her arms. "Such good news Sylvia sent me."

At once Colby understood her surprising appearance. Her Aunt Sylvia was in for a tremendous tongue-lashing for bringing the old lady down to the country at the most inopportune moment.

"Tell me, how is poor Matthew?" her mother-in-law inquired.

"He is not flourishing, but I think he is better than I found him," she said. "The doctor is not at all sanguine."

Colby hastened to have the London party settled so that she could start putting her plan in train. But she hadn't counted on Lady Miriam's happiness on becoming a grandmother again.

"Let me look at you?" she said, turning Colby from front to back, embarrassing Lear and the servants hovering nearby. Lady Browning was a firm believer that age had its privileges. One could be deliciously outrageous. "You look a treat, and I am very proud of you and Nevil."

Colby blushed every color of red.

"And where *is* that great lout of a son of mine, permitting you to travel alone to face this disaster by yourself?"

Colby swore under her breath. Why hadn't she sought a ready answer to the obvious question.

"He has some business to finish in Paris, and I was sickening for home."

Lady Miriam knew a lie when she heard one. Her shrewd sensibilities told her that Colby was laboring under great stress, and she suspected it was more than just her brother's accident, as terrible as that was.

"I shall freshen myself before coming to see Matthew," she announced airily.

"Surely your trip has worn you down?" Colby shot in, trying to keep her mother-in-law at a distance as long as she could. "Perhaps tomorrow morning would be a better time."

"Nonsense. I'm right as rain." Miriam Browning was not easily put off and a match for her daughter-in-law.

"Come, of course, but allow me to leave before you to pre-

pare the family for your visit." This time Colby meant to prevail, and Lady Miriam gave in with good grace.

Harvey Cortnage damned the day he ever threw in his lot
with Panaman. His city clothes were dirty and covered with
bracken. He was hungry and perishing for strong drink. He'd
ransacked the littered cave, but found nothing but a square of
hard cheese and a few apples. He heard footsteps. All he
needed was to have someone come upon him in Panaman's
lair.

"You've taken long enough," he lashed out, relieved to see
that it was Panaman after all.

"Hold your water," Panaman said, unloading two rabbits
from a stick over his shoulder. "And why the hell are you
here? Last time you said you'd never come back."

"Had to, Gus. I need to talk to you," he said, thinking it wise
to moderate his annoyance. Panaman's hair-trigger temper
needed careful handling

"Say your piece."

"Let's get out of England. I've got money enough to take us
anyplace. We can go to Australia, buy ourselves an empire if
we want." He was treading carefully and the effort cost him
dearly. Everything told him that Panaman was barely holding
on to his sanity. He opened the bag and emptied banknotes on
the earthen floor.

Panaman looked at the money, fingered a stack of bills, and
weighed Cortnage's offer. In the end he threw the money back
on the floor.

"Tell me something I don't know. I'm going to finish with
that bitch and her family tonight," he said, his eyes wild. "I've
been stalking her, and I'm ready for the kill."

"Don't be a fool," Cortnage screamed hysterically. "Browning's secretary is bringing his mother down here. You can't
sneak up on them this time."

"So much the better." Panaman was beside himself with
glee.

"You've had your revenge on her and all the money you
need to start anew. What more can you want?"

"Colby Browning is alive, isn't she?" Panaman asked, crouching to skin the rabbits.

"You're crazy, and I'm going to stop you, whatever it takes."

Panaman turned around, and in one lightning move lifted Cortnage as if the fat man were a sack of potatoes and hurled him headfirst against a wall of the cave. His face broken and bloodied, Cortnage looked with staring, unbelieving eyes as he slipped downward along the wall, moaning like a wounded animal. Panaman picked up a cudgel and brought it down on his head.

Chapter 39

Colby presided over the tea table, her nerves on end, willing the remainder of the day away. The best she could hope for was an early departure of her guests. Nothing on earth could deter her from postponing her search for Panaman. But she hadn't counted on Lady Miriam's robust good health and joy at being reunited with Sylvia Rainwriter, for whom she had taken a great liking during their short acquaintance in London.

Lear noted Colby's growing restiveness, her eyes swiveling every few minutes to the old carriage clock on the mantel. When everyone had been served, he sought an excuse to detach her.

"Lady Colby, could we talk about your plans for the estate?" he asked casually.

She rewarded him with a smile and led the way to the book room. Her aunt, still smarting from the sharp talking-to Colby had given her earlier, was only too pleased to have Lady Miriam to herself.

"Now tell me why you are shedding your skin?" Lear said when he closed the door on them. "You're bursting to be off someplace."

She launched into a brief explanation of her suspicions about Panaman and told him she was seeking further proof of villainy with help from Evans and his friend.

"I don't expect to find Panaman tonight, but I want to confirm to myself that he has been watching the house," she explained breathlessly. "I feel in my bones that he is not finished with us, but I don't plan to be taken by surprise again."

Lear held up his hand. "I know you hate to be reminded that you are a woman without protection, but Lord Nevil would never forgive me if I didn't try to caution you."

"John, don't be stupidly sentimental. You know how things stand between Lord Browning and me," she spat out.

"How do they stand?" It was Lady Miriam, standing in the doorway rigid and commanding. "Leave us, John."

She took a chair and without a word ordered Colby to take one next to her. "I am waiting for an answer."

Colby decided she was finished with evasions. "Nevil and I married to give you a grandchild to replace Robert." The words were out, and Colby felt better for it. The whole truth was worse and only to be kept locked away in her heart. "We feel nothing for each other."

Lady Miriam let that pass. Maybe her son was blind to this extraordinary woman. She would find that out for herself in due time. But her wise old eyes knew what they saw. Colby was anything but indifferent to Nevil.

"What of the baby?"

"I will raise the child in the country, and Nevil can resume the only life that suits him elsewhere."

"It is not an unheard of arrangement among my friends and their children, and if it suits you, I wish you happiness," Lady Miriam pronounced coldly. "And now, let us talk of Matthew. I have some suggestions to make."

Lady Miriam told Colby about Dr. William Lawrence of St. Bartholomew's Hospital in London, a noted and revered colleague of her own Dr. Corday.

"William is considered something of a miracle worker and a most celebrated surgeon. With your permission, I shall write and ask him to come here."

Colby slipped from her chair and lay her head in Lady Miriam's lap, hoping for the first time to let go some of the iron control in a flood of tears. The old woman smoothed back the thick, black hair and made the kinds of soothing sounds calculated to give sustenance to a troubled mind.

Under cover of night, Evans and Pierce arrived at the side door at Brawleigh and were received by Colby.

She saw that Pierce was a slight, old man, and her heart sank. There was nothing about him at first glance to instill confidence, until she saw his eyes burning with crafty intelligence.

She closed the curtains of a bare room near the door before lighting a small candle. She offered large glasses of whiskey to warm them against the biting cold outside.

"Thank you for coming."

"Couldn't keep me away," Shad Pierce said in his thick, country accent. "You think Panaman started the fire? Wouldn't put it past the bleeding beast."

Pierce pleased Colby more than he knew. He supported her feelings and stiffened her belief in her resolution.

"What do you suggest, Shad?" She plainly deferred to him in an attempt to bind him to her. He might after all be a worthy match for her prey, and his evident hatred of Panaman appeared to equal her own.

"I will find him."

"Can we start tonight?"

"You'd leave a track a baby could follow," he said, not bothering to hide his disgust.

"I insist on going with you," Colby said flatly. She had no intention of ceding her leadership.

"No." Pierce downed his drink and prepared to leave. He was a prickly man, so Evans had warned her, and now she believed him. The country thereabouts was full of such men, whose pride kept them outsiders, deaf to the entreaties of others to conform and a pathological dislike of the trappings of society. Colby knew when she was beaten and retreated as gracefully as she could.

"Will you start tonight then?" she asked pleadingly.

"Evans, you leave first from another part of the house, and you, mistress, go to bed. If I'm right, old Gussie is watching from somewhere, and he can't easily follow us if we go in different ways."

"When will you let me know what you have found?" Colby was unable to keep from pressing him and showing her high expectations, even though she knew Pierce was not to be dealt with like other men.

"When I'm good and ready."

Colby laughed and led Evans away. Pierce was as single-minded as she was herself, and she loved his great confidence in himself. At least tonight she could go to bed feeling safe for the first time since her return. And some of the despair that had invaded her spirit since she came home eased enough to enable her to sleep.

Toward daybreak she was awakened by a dream of Nevil, her body engulfed in moist warmth as demanding of fulfillment as any time in Paris when he came to her bed and satisfied her lust. She cringed in shame and frustration, curling into a ball, willing her body and heart to settle for a life without physical love.

"Colly, are you sick," Matthew called from his bed.

"It's nothing, darling," she called out. But it was everything.

Chapter 40

A driving storm designed to match his mood greeted Nevil on the last leg of his journey to London. Wet to his small-clothes, having refused to use his traveling coach, his staff bundled him indoors and into a long, hot soak in an ornate brass tub. A hot meal and a drink soon relieved his aching muscles, but eased little else. He begged for sleep, lolling in a great leather wing chair with long legs stretched toward a roaring fire. But his mind had a mind of its own and would do nothing but dwell on Moreton House and conjure up a picture of Colby and her family enjoying its comforts.

He freely acknowledged his cowardice. He wanted to be with her, to earn her love more than he had ever wanted anything in the world. The hell of war was nothing to the dread he would feel if those lovely amethyst eyes, which could depress the ambitions of the devil, were to stare him down and order him from his own home. And she would do it without turning a hair.

She had made it as plain as the nose on his face. She wanted nothing more to do with him. She was repelled by him, but nothing he knew could fill the void she had created in his life when she left Paris so precipitously.

Every stratagem he had devised since had been stupid, born of desperation, and discarded as less than useless. Colby would not care how many dragons he slew, how many romantic poems he composed, he told himself. She would walk a mile to avoid a trove of jewels strewn at her feet. Other women might have given him a hearing, but not Colby. To her he would always be the insensitive lout from the first day they met, and that portrait would remain no matter what he did to change it.

He could appease the angriest of gods more easily than he could move her. From wanting her love, he had descended down the scale of dreams to asking for a place in her life, to adore her from afar. But not too far. He had thought that Gracia had left him riven and ruined, but the way he felt about the loss of Colby was in the same case as his grief for Robert, his sister, and the death of his father combined in one. How in God's name had this come to pass, he asked himself for the hundredth time.

Nevil knew he had to call a halt and go to his club. He needed immediate diversion and a steep game of hazard, the company of his more frivolous friends, the opiates he had used so effectively to cure himself of Gracia and the bloodiness of war in what seemed an age ago.

He arrived at White's an hour later and was greeted like the lost prodigal. Mercifully, his depression left him in the haze of smoke and good cheer, the noise of tinkling glasses, and the staccato of gambling counters. It was not heaven, but it would do for the moment.

Glassy-eyed with fatigue, mellowed by drink, and mildly pleased with vowels and paper money, which stood like a small pyramid before him on the card table, it took time to realize that Tarn Maitland was at his elbow ready to take him away from the play.

Maitland pointed to a small grouping of chairs far from the card room. His face was grave, but he wouldn't explain himself until they had been served drinks and cigars.

"You took your sweet time getting back," Tarn said.

"You've had all my reports," Nevil responded, drinking deeply.

"Then why weren't you back sooner?"

"Too complicated to say." Nevil dogged the question. The whole world didn't have to know what a failure he was.

"Love bitten, aren't you?" Tarn said, taking note of the black rings under his friend's eyes, the thin face, and air of melancholy.

"And what is that in aid of?" Nevil asked, his hackles showing, but cautious to the last.

"Barbara said all along that you were probably going to fall
arse over tea kettle for your bride, but probably wouldn't know
it."

Browning was about to tell him to go to hell when the need
to confide in someone won over his natural distaste for baring
his feelings.

"Barbara sees too much and too well, thank you very
much."

"What are you going to do about it?"

"Colby would use my guts for tennis if she had the chance.
I'm doing damn all nothing."

Tarn examined his perfect fingernails trying to decide how
much to tell him. "Colby needs you, but she wouldn't like me
saying that." Maitland decided to test his friend. "I've had letters from your mother and John Lear, and Bill Lawrence is on
his way to Brawleigh."

Nevil was fair to pulling Maitland out of his chair to beat
the whole story out of him. "Is Colby ill?"

Maitland gave him a long explanation of what had happened
since Colby's return from France.

"I'm leaving."

"Not without me." Tarn rose and took Nevil by the arm. A
racing curricle of the latest design waited at the door. Maitland, as usual, was two steps ahead of everyone.

Chapter 41

Lady Miriam didn't know what troubled her most, the way her daughter-in-law was becoming more thin and taut to the point of breaking, or Matthew, who lay listless, half in and half out of consciousness. Her daily visits were becoming a trial.

"Sylvia, I tell you disaster hangs over this house," the old lady said during luncheon at Brawleigh one afternoon. "Colby is distracted, always seeming to be waiting for something that doesn't happen."

"I've tried to talk to her, but she won't listen," Sylvia said, ringing her hands. "She's up before the maids and asleep long after midnight. What will become of her and the baby?"

Soon after, Colby and John Lear came in from a brisk ride around the estate with the builders, determining what needed to be done to the tenant cottages. The estate rang with hammers and men hurrying to and fro over the roofs and through the cellars.

"Has anyone sent a message for me?" Colby inquired, the same question she asked whenever she returned.

The old women shook their heads.

"Drat the man."

"What is it that's troubling you now?" Lady Miriam asked, making it clear she was not to be fobbed off.

"Nothing to upset you," Colby hastened to reply. She didn't intend to confide in anyone, and waiting for word from Pierce was becoming impossibly difficult. She had badgered Evans, but the manager was at a loss to explain Shad's unaccountable silence. They'd come to the same conclusion: Panaman had found Pierce before Shad found him. It was too terrible to think about.

Colby made her excuses and hurried to look in on Matthew. The ointment she'd made from the resin had improved the burns, but it was too slight to satisfy her. Matthew continued to suffer, reluctant to complain and upset the household and Lady Miriam, who was in and out at all hours. Colby was steeling herself to talk to Dr. Reed, who was not at all pleased by her temerity in using something he had not himself introduced. The stench of rotting flesh in the room threatened another siege of nausea, and she knew what the smell augured, worsening gangrene.

Colby stayed with her brother, holding his hand and telling him things she knew he wanted to hear. John Lear had promised to find a tutor to prepare him and Mark for Eton, and when the workmen were done he would have a small study of his own, something his solitary nature required.

Matthew was so much like her father, his head forever in a book, happy to lose himself in another world. She wanted to tell him about the doctor that Lady Miriam had summoned, but Dr. Lawrence hadn't appeared or written, and she was afraid to raise his expectations. It was enough that she was beside herself, unable to see any relief at the end of the road. They heard sounds of horses and men's voices in the hall, and she promised to come back as soon as she dealt with the intrusion. The last thing she needed was more guests.

The sight of Nevil, Tarn Maitland, and another man in the hall surrounded by Lady Miriam, her aunt, and Mark, all talking at once, sent the blood rushing to her head, and she had to hold on to the wall to steady herself. He had come. He had heard her prayers, and if she could move, if he gave her a sign, she would throw herself into his arms. He would fix everything. Her Viking.

Nevil saw Colby over the heads of the others. Despite the peaked look on her face, the faded riding clothes, she was more magnificent, more woman than he remembered. He ached to lift the burdens she had shouldered alone and too long. He made his way toward her, and she went to meet him.

"This house is cursed, and I am taking you to Moreton where you belong, whether you like it or not."

She stared at him dumbly. How she had wanted his strength, wanted him near, but once again her heart had played tricks on her, her yearnings brought the ill fortune she encountered at every turn.

What she saw was the same peremptory, domineering Nevil Browning of their first disastrous meeting. This was not the man she had idolized and made Godlike in her dreams since returning from Paris. She was being cheated again, and she exploded in disappointment.

"How dare you come here and take over our lives." She wanted to scream, but kept her voice low and harsh. She couldn't allow their private war to unsettle the household any more than it was. "I have taken care of my family and will continue to do so. How many times have I told you that Moreton can never be my home, and if Brawleigh is not to your liking, too bad. I don't want you here."

The others stood about, not knowing what transpired, but well aware that Nevil and Colby were coming to cuffs. It was left to Tarn Maitland to bring them to their senses.

"My dear Colby, how remiss of me to leave Dr. Lawrence waiting to see his patient."

At once a subdued Colby greeted the doctor with gratitude for answering their need and showed him into the drawing room.

The difference between Dr. Lawrence and the country butcher, as she called Dr. Reed, was astonishing. The London consultant was gentle and consoling, distracting Matthew with practiced patter as easily as if he'd known the boy for years. The examination was swift and sure, and Dr. Lawrence's expertness was apparent in seconds even to Colby's untrained eye.

"Where did you find this ointment, my dear?"

"I could not find gum trees here," she said nervously. "Cherry trees had to do, and I am afraid it was a poor substitute."

Dr. Lawrence smiled encouragingly.

"I made the ointment loosely based on an entry from a diary

my father kept on his experiences of native medicine during his army service in India."

"That explains it," the doctor said approvingly. "I am familiar with the Ayurvedic medical system and use it often on my own patients. Lady Miriam was most explicit, and I brought some gum resin and other medicants with me."

Colby breathed a sigh of relief. It had been an act of madness countering Dr. Reed's orders. Now she could breathe easier knowing she hadn't harmed Matthew after all.

"I am going to give you something to make you sleep, Matthew," he said gently. "Don't worry. I shall be here for a while."

The doctor pointed toward the door, and Colby followed to where the family and Maitland awaited them.

"The leg is gangrenous and ill-knit, but I have no doubt that matters would have been even more dire if Lady Browning had not interceded," Lawrence said, patting Colby's arm reassuringly.

"Dr. Reed wanted to amputate the leg. Was I wrong in delaying that?" Colby was still gray with guilt at another example of her high-handedness.

All could see that Dr. Lawrence was in a quandary and looked for rescue to Nevil and Tarn.

"Talk to me," Colby insisted, irritated that, like all males, the doctor looked for guidance from men.

"You misread me, my dear," he hastened to say. "I dislike passing judgment on a colleague, especially a rural one. Some doctors are too quick to amputate rather than let medicines and nature determine the course."

"My wife is impatience itself," Nevil said, trying to apologize for Colby's insult, again putting himself in the wrong. "Please give us your diagnosis."

"I need more time, but I think that if Matthew is strong enough and I have the skill, he will come about."

Colby knew Dr. Lawrence was equivocating, and her disenchantment was so terrible that it made her feel faint.

Seeing her falter, Dr. Lawrence caught her before she fell. Nevil scooped her up in his arms and mounted the staircase two steps at a time and set her down on the first bed he came upon. The doctor followed him.

"I think you should know, William, that my wife is with child," Nevil said, still smarting from Colby's rejection. "You must tell her she needs the help of others."

"Pour a drink for me, Nevil. That's a good lad," he said teasingly, ushering him to the door. He came back and sat down on the bed.

"I don't recommend all this turmoil for a lady in your state," he said, examining her gently.

"Tell that to the Fates, Doctor," Colby said bitterly. "In addition to my brother's unfortunate accident, there is a man out there waiting to kill me and my family."

"Yes, I know. Nevil told me when we met by chance on the road coming here," Dr. Lawrence said, all sympathy. "I will do all I can to help your brother, and you must allow your husband and Captain Maitland to deal with that maniac. And you, my dear, must only be concerned for your child."

"You don't know me very well, Dr. Lawrence," Colby sneered. "I do not delegate my responsibilities."

"I have a fair idea of your nature and extraordinary capabilities," he said wryly, choosing his words, "but pigheadedness isn't a virtue either."

Colby laughed. She began to like the man enormously after all. He understood all her difficulties, probably did not approve of her intransigence, but didn't condemn her either.

"I see no cause for alarm, Lady Browning, but I must caution you to do things in moderation," he said when he finished the examination. "You are made to bear children and will deliver Nevil a healthy child. But don't tempt fate. You are worn thin and need rest."

Colby nodded and thanked him. An afternoon nap, usually an anathema to her, suddenly seemed the most natural thing to do. She was asleep almost before the doctor left.

He made his way downstairs and gathered all but Mark into the morning room.

"Young Matthew is in a bad state," he said solemnly. "I did not want to say this in Lady Colby's hearing, but saving the leg is highly problematic."

Nevil stole into the bedroom and sat in the chair next to the bed, watching Colby sleep, his heart in his eyes. It was the first time he had ever seen her so unguarded since the night on his yacht. Why is peace and understanding so difficult between us, he asked himself, more hopelessly in love with her than ever.

He was still smarting from a session with his mother and Sylvia Rainwriter, after giving them a highly edited version of what had happened between them in the hall. He couldn't escape the notion that he had made a grievous miscalculation. Would he never learn that Colby could not be dictated to and must always go her own way?

"Why do I feel that you were cow-handed with Colby?" his mother asked, reading between the lines. Her son took after her, direct to a fault, and would never be the diplomat his father was.

"Brawleigh, dear Nevil, has always been a totem for Colby," Miss Rainwriter explained in her graceful way. "Her father loved the place and talked longingly of returning here. It became a symbol, a beacon of sorts, while she was growing up in India."

He went back to studying his sleeping wife.

"What the devil are you doing here?" Colby woke, startled to see him so close.

"I came to make peace, at least until Panaman is caught and Matthew is feeling more the thing," he said lamely.

"How many times must I tell you that I don't need your help?" she stormed, rejecting his hand as he made to help her off the bed.

"I agree you don't need anyone, and I promise I'll go away quietly when the danger passes," he said, trying to be reasonable. "Surely you can use Tarn and me in whatever you're plotting."

"How do you know I'm plotting anything?" She was instantly on the offensive. Had Shad Pierce sent word while she slept?

"You would never sit still under Panaman's threat and allow yourself and the family to be targets without some plan in that agile brain of yours." Nevil decided that his mother was right.

A little guile with his wife might turn her up sweet. Might was always the operative word with Colby.

She prowled the room, wondering how much to tell him about Pierce. That long rest had refreshed her. She was satisfied that she had given Nevil as good as she got when he came charging in ready to take over and shunt her aside like some kind of hothouse flower. The very thought of that moment sent her into the boughs. Still he came back for more.

Why? Suddenly Nevil's motive were clear to her. He wasn't interested in anything except saving his child and heir. That would explain his telling Dr. Lawrence about his concern for the baby. Hadn't Lady Miriam let slip that the Browning estate could be inherited by a woman? Even if her baby was a girl, the Browning inheritance would be secure. Why should that surprise me, Colby argued with herself. Right from the beginning, Nevil's only concern has been the continuation of the Browning line. She was seething.

Nevil watched her, marveling at the air of life and independence she gave off. Even when the odds were against her, she wanted to go her own way.

Colby was a rare woman, and he, a fool from the start, hadn't the wit to see it. A man would need nothing else in his life if he could win Colby's love and esteem. What a slow top I was to have demeaned her and sent her away like common baggage that first time. With all his wealth, with all his lineage, he had nothing if he didn't have Colby and their baby. The prospect of life without her was becoming more and more bleak.

Colby saw none of this, too absorbed in the few choices left to her as she saw it. Panaman was probably at that very moment spying on them, and Pierce proved a frail reed to rely on. She could join forces with Nevil or continue to go it alone. Colby wasn't sure what the right thing to do was anymore.

"Let us go below, and I will tell you and Captain Maitland what I am about," Colby said, reluctant to the end.

The three were closeted in the spare room where she had met Pierce and Evans the week before.

"I don't know if Pierce is alive or dead," she said at the conclusion of her recital, sickened by the thought of his fate. "He is a curmudgeon of the first water and takes his own road."

"If Evans doesn't know where he is, could someone else tell us something?" Tarn asked.

"I told you, Pierce only acts for himself," Colby said, exasperated, as if he were a retarded child.

"Look, Colby, if Panaman is angry with you for the whipping, he must hate my guts for having run him off the estate," Nevil reasoned. "I mean to go after him."

Colby's first thought was fear for Nevil, who by no stretch of imagination could cope with Panaman's prowess and killing skills in the wild. She deplored her sudden concern for his safety. She must not let down her guard again. Nevil was nothing to her. Nothing!

Tarn Maitland studied them. His knowledge of the world enabled him to see more than most. He could understand the patently obvious war of wills between these two uncompromising, implacable people. Hadn't he and Barbara, before their marriage, been prime examples of that special breed who deluded themselves into thinking they knew the right and wrong of everything.

Earlier, Lady Miriam told him all she'd gleaned of the way things stood between Nevil and Colby, and Maitland could see the old lady wasn't much off the mark. He decided to take a hand in breaking the impasse.

"We should all think more on this," he said in his deep, authoritarian baritone. "The key is to make Panaman believe this is just a jolly reunion of the clan, until we hear from that scout of yours."

The proposal appealed to Colby and Nevil, and the meeting broke up.

Panaman sought in vain for a time and place to wipe out the two families, and his mind contrived and discarded a host of schemes. Another fire was out of the question. With Cortnage dead and moldering in the cave, he had no one to help him. Besides, it went against the grain to repeat himself.

Picking them off one by one was too easy, not enough sport

in that for him. But he didn't mean to take too much time in achieving his ends.

He was sitting in a second bolt hole he'd built and equipped in case someone spied out the cave a quarter of a mile away. As if anyone could take *him* unawares. He emptied the dead pipe he'd been smoking, took a long swig from the bottle of whiskey he'd stolen from Moreton on his last raid, and incidentally priding himself on the frequency of those forays. When he was running the place, no one would have dared steal a pin, much less all the stores he carried away at will. He and Cortnage had looted Moreton for years, and no one had been the wiser.

He had never been as lax as Evans. He had kept a tight rein on every single Browning possession as if it were his own. And wasn't everything his by rights? Hadn't he taken it from a neglected, secondary gentleman's residence to an estate of plenty? He had joyfully made himself feared worse than purgatory, grown strong seeing the staff and tenants shrink and crawl at the sight of him. Then that bitch took against him, and his fiefdom collapsed.

He would not give up so easily again and saw himself as invincible. All he needed to complete his life was the annihilation of the Mannerings and Brownings. He would move contentedly on after that with the money Cortnage had given him.

Panaman's ears perked up. All bird and animal sounds shifted pitch at once. Someone was near. His hearing, as acute as any animal's, had saved him too many times to question. The same was true of his extraordinary sense of smell. He picked up his long gun, stowed a knife and a dueling pistol in his belt, and crept out of the hole by a different way. He left nothing to chance.

He waited until the bird song resumed and made his way around to the opposite opening. Off in the distance he spied a man crouching and running, his clothes painted like a mat of leaves on the forest floor. He knew that was Shad Pierce's trick. The bastard. What brought his old enemy this far from home?

Panaman's first thought was to stop him, but that would

mean two corpses on his hands. His only chance was that Shad had come upon him unknowingly, hadn't sussed out his other lair. To go after him or worse, lose him would be dangerous. The only other way anyone could track him was Jenny, his little mountain pony kept at the blind and deaf woman's scrubby farm. She was deemed a witch, and no one wanted to go near. That's why he had chosen her. For a few pennies she cared for the horse and let him in her bed whenever he liked. She didn't know who he was from Adam.

His reflexes, honed to danger and threat, made him run down all the possibilities that would account for Pierce's appearance.

Next to Colby Browning, Panaman hated and feared Pierce. He was the only man who could best him as a woodsman, the only man who had the nerve to call him a coward and walk away whole. These were terrible admissions for Panaman, and they stoked his mania.

Panaman's diseased mind made the leap that bridged his two worst enemies in a compact to kill him. Any way he looked at it, Colby must have sought out Pierce, or the other way round. They detested him enough, or possibly Cortnage was missed, and in a search for his whereabouts, someone came across evidence that the two were in league. It didn't make a particle of difference. His belief in himself was shaken, badly.

Panaman's premonition of danger made him cast about for answers, and needing to vent his frustration as only he knew, he swung his gun against a tree, splintering it as he had Cortnage's head. The action released a knot of doubt that had gripped him.

Chapter 42

Colby came in from her morning inspection of the builders' progress, laughing and holding Mark by the hand.

With her usual intensity, she had been correcting a terrible omission over the past few days. For soon after Nevil arrived she had become aware that her younger brother was being terribly neglected and denied his share of her attention. She had seen him hanging on to Nevil for dear life, listening to every word as if it were gospel. She soon put a stop to that, and now Mark rarely left her side.

Colby's step was lighter and her face, free of strain, was pink with robust health. She had reason to be pleased for the first time in an age. Matthew's leg had been reset properly, and his fever had come down. Dr. Lawrence was indeed the miracle worker that Lady Miriam had promised. The house was beginning to look spruce and cared for and on its way to the glory she had imagined when her father spoke of his idyllic childhood at Brawleigh.

But pleasure, she had learned early, was not without pain. Panaman was still free and beyond her reach, and Pierce still had not been heard from by anyone.

And Nevil. He moved silently on the periphery, never again questioning her authority or any of her ideas, usually in grave conversation with John Lear or conferring earnestly with Tarn Maitland. At meals taken at Brawleigh or Moreton, he sat silent, almost brooding, at the end of the table.

She should have been content, but she wasn't. Would she ever be? The simple truth was every time she saw Nevil she was reminded of the day of his return, when her heart dropped to her shoes, when he seemed to open his arms to her, and the overwhelming need she felt to lose herself and shelter herself against his heart. It had been close, a near thing. That day she was more overburdened than ever, and she would have let him share her miseries if he hadn't spoiled it all and become the imperial Nevil Browning of their first meeting. It came to her that silence was indeed golden, and if people didn't have tongues, life would be sweeter.

She didn't like the way her mind was heading, and she went to check on Matthew. He was playing cards with Nevil, his eyes clear and eager, a far cry from the way he looked before Dr. Lawrence had come.

"Colly, Nevil is showing me how to play cards," he called out.

Colby was beside herself. "I would have thought, my lord, that you of all people would not want to perpetuate the Mannering curse," Colby exploded. "And you, Matthew, know how I feel about gaming."

The two looked sheepish, but that didn't wash with her.

"Lord Nevil has offered to send me and Mark to the school he has started for some of the sons of men and officers who fought in the Peninsula with Wellington."

Colby's eyes blazoned. "You are going to Eton. Papa said the regret of his life was that he didn't have a decent classical education at Sandhurst, and he wanted you and Mark to make up for his deficiencies."

She continued to glower at Nevil. Without lifting a finger, her husband was undermining her influence with the boys, and she would have to put a stop to it at once.

"My lord, please join me for a stroll." The invitation was given with little expectation of pleasure for either of them. Nevil, none too pleased, followed her through the French doors overlooking the back lawn.

If he thought he had seen Colby in a tear before, it was nothing to the harsh way she addressed him when they were alone.

"How dare you subvert my influence with my brothers," Colby yelled, making no effort to keep this quarrel from the workmen scurrying about. "I have their lives mapped, and I don't appreciate your twopenny interference."

Nevil's face darkened, and he took her by the elbow and piloted her across the lawn out of range of inquisitive ears.

"I am sick and tired of your jumping to conclusions," he fought back, showing a side that had frightened many a raw recruit and cowered people who overstepped the mark. It was having a similar effect on Colby.

"If you had listened, you might have learned that Browning's chief reason for existence is to give a leg up to boys who haven't had the social or educational advantages as others fighting for places at Eton, Oxford, and Cambridge," he said heatedly.

"You are nothing more than crammers," Colby said dismissively. "I can get those aplenty."

"If it gives you pleasure to deprecate me, go ahead and enjoy yourself." Nevil had long since given up trying to reach her. "You may be very smart and very devoted to your family, but you must allow me to say that you don't know a goddamned thing about a boy's proper education and may do them a great deal of harm. Think on it."

Nevil moved away. He'd had enough and was afraid of what he might say next. Besides, he'd given her something to think about.

"Just a moment," Colby called after him. He'd hit a nerve, and even her vaunted pride and hatred of advice wouldn't go so far as to risk hurting her brothers' future.

"What did you mean?" She'd taken his arm and made him stop.

Nevil's first thought was to throw off her hand, but the touch of her conjured up images he had still not been able to conquer.

"Young boys don't give a fig about great names and property. Real life corrupts them later," he said sadly. "They do care about their school friendships. They want to be with a chap who knows all the right jokes, the current fads and foibles of the schoolboy, the right manners, and dress. They want friends who are good at games and are sportsmen, and a host of things you could never have a clue about."

Colby groaned. Of course, I didn't know all that, she chided herself. She was getting an education, and she didn't like it one bit that Nevil, of all people, was her teacher.

"Wouldn't their connection with your name obviate all that?"

"You still don't really understand, do you?" And this time Nevil was not quite so blinded by Colby's undeniable physical hold over him. She had married him as coldly as he had married her, and she thought herself safe from the world. He would have felt sorry for her if he didn't feel utterly defeated by his own early delusions about their marriage. *And what the hell am I doing arguing the finer points of public school life with this firebrand, who hates me and everything I stand for?*

"Your brothers have had little contact with boys their own ages. I can open doors for them later, but to be successes at Eton or University they need to make lifelong friends, which will mean more to them now than my name or money. Individualism is all well and good, but the important thing to a boy in his first years at school is conformity and acceptance. Boys are capable of the most monstrous behavior if another boy doesn't pass muster. Do you want your brothers to be called freaks?"

"How does Browning's make a difference?" she asked, incredulous once again by all that she didn't know about her husband's life before she married him.

"We prepare a boy in every way to make the run for placement in the great schools. If he can't make the grade, we keep him and give him a good education and practical skills to make his way in life. Many of our boys are simply not scholars."

Colby was ashamed of herself. Again she thought, *I've mistaken the power of money. I thought it solved everything.*

Nevil wasn't in the least convinced that he had made a dent in Colby's understanding, but he was glad that he'd done what was right for his young brothers-in-law. Whatever she decided and however much she deplored it, Nevil knew he would watch over them as if they were his own sons. In the past few days they had completely won his heart. If Colby did half as good a job on their own child, he could rest easy, and much as he might hate it, he would keep his word and his distance and watch her raise his heir from afar. Hadn't events proved she would never relinquish anything that was hers, no matter how hard he tried to redeem himself in her eyes? And worse, in her heart.

He went to find Tarn Maitland.

In disgust with all the inaction she had imposed on him, his forbearance in dealing with Panaman was wearing thin. He no longer intended to do things Colby's way.

As soon as Panaman was captured, Nevil decided, he would return to London and set about planning an extended trip of the world, the Grand Tour, in fact, that Napoleon had robbed him of in his youth. The only question remaining was, should he start before or after the birth of his child?

Colby had fallen into a troubled sleep, and the appearance of a man in her bedroom scared the life out of her, especially as Nevil and Tarn had him unarmed and wrestled to the ground before she got the sleep out of her eyes.

"What's happening?" she asked, lighting the candle near the bed.

"You don't think we'd let anyone kill you in your bed?" Nevil said, about to march the intruder out of the room.

"Leave him. He is Shad Pierce," she cried out.

"Damn it, man, you're as good as your reputation," Nevil said, impressed. "That explains why we didn't detect you sooner."

Tarn picked him off the floor and made as if to dust him off, apologizing profusely.

"Why don't we go down and have a drink while my wife makes herself presentable."

Colby hurried out of bed. "Don't tell them anything, Shad, until I get there."

She found them in the kitchen sitting over whiskey and sandwiches, the place looking like a tornado had struck.

Colby laughed.

"We had to do something waiting for your appearance,"

Nevil said lamely. "Now that her ladyship is here, you can tell us what you've learned."

In his terse, country way, Pierce told them he had tracked Panaman to an ingeniously hidden, old Druid cave outfitted for a long siege.

"I made a terrible discovery. He's got a rotting body there, and I found this."

Nevil reached for the wallet that Pierce produced.

"Harvey Cortnage, by God," Nevil said, emptying the contents. There were two sets of travel papers and a receipt from a bank showing a sizable withdrawal.

"Cortnage was always making excuses for Panaman. But what could they have in common?" Nevil wondered aloud.

"They were bleeding you blind, and you never knew it," Colby replied roughly. "Ask anyone. Moreton is the most successful estate for fifty miles around, and the ledgers of Panaman's time do not reflect it. You couldn't know, because you didn't deign to visit."

Browning felt like a mug. One day, if she ever gave him the opportunity, he would tell her the legacy that until now shrouded his memories of Moreton. It was here that he came a broken man after Badajoz and Gracia wrought havoc on him. Would she ever listen? Would she ever want to understand? He didn't think Colby ever doubted the future and cursed the fates as he had in his long, lonely exile at Moreton.

It was left to Maitland to intervene and bring Nevil around to the present.

"That doesn't tell us where Panaman is now, does it, Pierce?"

The old woodsman agreed.

"I wrecked the cave, and I have a fair idea where he might be."

"You didn't see him then?" Colby was on the edge of her chair. "He's still roaming free?"

"Now he knows someone is after him, what do you think he will do?" Nevil asked.

"If it were me, I'd take that little mountain pony he keeps at the witch's place and be off like a shot."

"But you don't think he's going to do that?" Nevil asked, catching Shad's drift at once.

"Stands to reason," Pierce said. "I never took a penny of the money in the saddlebags. He's biding his time for somethin'."

The others had a fair idea what Panaman was plotting.

"I think subtlety is wasted on Mr. Panaman," Nevil said at last, and the look on his face was anything but subtle. "Tarn, please escort Colby back to her room."

Nevil's voice left no room for Colby to doubt he would not take kindly to any refusal of hers. Maitland, who knew how to handle headstrong women, escorted Colby to her bedroom.

"I think you and my wife are the most admirable, courageous women I know, but there comes a time, with respect, Colby, when your presence is a hindrance," he said gently. "Trust your husband, no matter what your feelings for him. His concerns are for you, your family, and his mother, and he can't think properly if you divert his mind with arguments, challenges, and what you consider your better generalship."

It was not in Colby to be gainsaid by anyone, and she began to protest. But Tarn wasn't finished with her, and he was a man she respected enormously.

"Lady Browning, have faith that others are as capable and as single-minded as yourself," he said, his eyes showing he had no intention of coddling her further. "And something else. This is an imperfect world, and maybe that will change one day. But in the year 1820, men are more likely to lay down their lives for a man who has led other men in battle and survived than for an untried woman, no matter what her capabilities."

Maitland finally made the only argument that could silence Colby. She had seen too much of the mysteries of army life not to realize all that went into gauging and understanding one's enemy and the strength and weaknesses of one's own forces. Besides, Maitland was a man who exuded confidence like a musk, and what he said next settled any remaining doubts.

"Nevil was one of the most resourceful and highly regarded junior officers in Wellington's army, and the Duke told me so himself. Nev's a match for Augustus Panaman, woodsman or no woodsman."

He took Colby to her door, kissed her hand, and bade her good night.

Maitland returned to find Nevil animated, with drawings and plans all over the table before him.

"Tarn, this is what we are going to do," he said, as Pierce looked on in admiration. "We are going to make a noisy attack on Panaman tomorrow morning, and with a flank movement around the mute's farm as well."

"But Shad wrecked the cave, and Panaman would be a fool to stay nearby," Tarn pointed out.

"I don't give a damn where he is, I just want him to know we are going after him in force," Browning said, smiling broadly. "I want him driven to distraction and off guard until I can finish our other plan. Keeping him away from Brawleigh for a few days is the key to everything."

"In the meantime, I will try to find his second bolt hole, and, according to Lord Nevil's plan, show Panaman that I've found it and know where it is. That will drive him batty, if I am any judge of the man," Pierce said gleefully.

"You don't talk of capturing him?" Tarn was puzzled.

"At the moment that's asking too much. He's too wily," Nevil explained. "My father always said, when you overestimate an opponent, you've outthought him, and you won't be taken by surprise if he does the unexpected."

Maitland agreed and looked forward to the next day's adventure.

Augustus Panaman finished trimming his beard and mustache and allowed the farm woman to cut the back of his hair according to his hand signals. He was certain he looked totally unlike his former self and was proud of his handiwork. He was thirty pounds slimmer, his hair, no longer dyed, had come out mouse gray. He had blackened two front teeth and wore spectacles. He was sure he could pass as an itinerant carpenter.

Pierce's foray into the land near his second hideout had made him go back to the cave. Shad had done a better job than he knew. Panaman went berserk. When he stopped raving, he racked his brains trying to figure out how he could accomplish the most destruction of the Mannerings and Brownings before they came after him with an army. That he was being hunted was no longer in doubt, and it made him even more determined to destroy his tormentors.

A few days earlier, his powerful field glassed had spied Nevil and Colby in a fierce argument on the terrace in the midst of workmen, whom from a distance looked like a rioting beehive. Studying them in relation to the workmen and the progress of the work being done on Brawleigh gave him an idea. He recognized few of the laborers as local men, which would make his job easier. That night he waylaid and killed a workman who was much like him in appearance and took his clothes, papers, and tools.

At dawn the next morning, on his way to Brawleigh to ask to be taken on as a carpenter, he spotted Nevil and Tarn leading a dozen men out of the barns, armed to the teeth and making enough noise to wake the dead.

Panaman wavered in which direction to take his vendetta. If he stayed at Brawleigh under the guise of a workman, he could decimate Colby's family, and, with luck, haul Lady Miriam in his net as well when she arrived for her daily visit. On the other hand, since his hatred of Nevil Browning was equal to his hatred of Colby, they both loomed large in his plans. But he knew he had to think that Browning would never rest until he got him for killing his wife and mother. It was not a comfortable dilemma. The question was, Panaman asked himself, what do I do first, go after the dragon's head or tail?

Nevil and Tarn had taken the high ground to watch their men disburse according to plan.

"I admire your tactics, but I'm not sure they are going to work," Tarn muttered.

"I'm not either, but I've lain awake nights trying to put myself in his boots," Browning said ruefully. "The problem is, I'm not crazy enough."

"It's better than sitting around doing nothing, at all odds."

"Well, I'm finished sitting around," Nevil said, dismounting and stripping off his rough hunting jacket in favor of a red sweater that could be seen from a distance.

"What the hell are you doing?"

"The real point in all this is making myself the biggest target I can be."

"You're out of your mind!"

Nevil laughed. "I'm still trying to think like a madman, don't you see? If I were Panaman, I'd hate my guts. I threw him off the best job a man like him could have, a sinecure, in fact, and I married and begot an heir with the woman who started his downfall. In his case, I'd want to destroy all of those who brought my comedown, and so would you, Tarn."

"This is suicidal," Maitland protested, standing up in his saddle.

"Hardly. I damn near have an army watching over me."

Browning was starting to descend the hill on foot when a series of rifle shots splattered over him with deadly accuracy, anticipating the angle his body would take down the slope. One of the bullets stopped Nevil's progress, as gunfire broke out in every direction where the tiny army had been positioned, waiting for Panaman to attack, and, if not, to make as much noise as possible.

Panaman, his carpenter's clothes shed in favor of buckskin, watched Nevil lying dead still in the underbrush, his own body shaking in a fever. I got the head, he gloated, and I'm after the tail, Panaman told himself, all the while ready to flee the treetop from where he had been watching his enemies from a safe vantage point.

"Stay still, Gussie. I got you in my sights." It was Shad Pierce, happy and flushed with the sense of long-deferred pleasure.

Panaman swore and dropped his field glasses, momentarily deflecting Shad's attention, but long enough for him to shoot with one hand and throw a knife with the other.

Colby never knew why, but she begged Dr. Lawrence to stay one more day, despite Matthew's continued progress. Bill Lawrence had wanted to be off and back to London to see to his other patients. He had been determined, in fact, until Lady Miriam added her pleas.

Suspecting that something was going on, Colby waited all day to hear from Nevil and Tarn, beside herself with annoyance because she hadn't been made privy to the plans she was sure the men had been devising a few nights before. She meant to correct that as soon as she saw them. She would never be excluded again.

A festive cream tea brought the household to Matthew's couch, where they were all in the best of cheer, when they heard terrible cries from the drive outside the house. Coming over the brow of the hill was Nevil and Tarn's rag-tag army carrying two makeshift litters.

Colby was the first out the door, running wildly and looking about herself frantically. She saw Tarn, but no Nevil, and her fears gave her the impetus to weave among the men and horses toward the first litter.

Shad Pierce lay ashen and cursing with rough, dirty bandages seeping with blood on his head and stomach. She took his hand and squeezed it in sympathy.

"We'll take care of you, don't worry," she murmured, all the time searching for a sign of her husband.

"I had Panaman, and I didn't kill him, mistress." Real tears made map lines down Pierce's wizened face.

"Next time," Colby said consolingly, just before cutting across to where Tarn and others were carrying the second pallet.

It was Nevil, lying gray-faced, hair matted and a large bandage on his right side. Tarn ordered the men to lower him. Colby bent down, keening in fear, covering Nevil's face with kisses.

"How could you go without me?" she wailed, silently calling on all the gods in heaven to keep Nevil alive. "It's my fault. I drove you . . ."

Nevil opened his eyes and stared at her in disbelief. "Tarn, I'm hallucinating, or worse off than you told me." Browning laughed, coughed, and clutched his side, but still he made to get up, and it took the combined strength of Colby and Tarn to keep him down.

Nevil took Colby's hand and held on for dear life, putting into his grasp all the love he had bottled up inside him. Somehow Colby understood and in her touch told him all his heart wanted to know. They couldn't keep their eyes off each other as Nevil was carried toward the house.

Dr. Lawrence was busy plying between Shad Pierce, whose wounds were serious, and Nevil's, which were minor.

"Panaman's bullet just grazed my side. Why is everyone making a war story out of it," Nevil protested. A steady stream of family and guests led by Colby and his mother hovered over him. "I am getting up for dinner, no matter what any of you say."

With Dr. Lawrence's agreement that the wound was superficial, Colby was beside herself with joy and went about the house beaming, even the threat of Panaman taking second place. As soon as she had seen to food and drink for the men who had gone in search of Panaman and had made sure that Pierce was being well nursed and as comfortable as possible, she stole back to her room, where she had insisted that Nevil be taken when he returned that morning. She closed the door on the last of his well-wishers and turned, suddenly shy.

"Now tell me what I want to hear, you vixen," Nevil said, holding his arms out.

Colby came into them, grateful to find at last the safe harbor she had been looking for all her life.

"Repeat after me." She laughed, always the rebel, but this time with shining eyes. "I love you as much as Colby loves me."

"I love and adore you," he said, pulling her closer, breathing into her wonderful ebony hair endearments he never thought to say to her in the darkest days of their strange marriage.

Colby lay content against him, afraid to believe that this wasn't another of the dreams that had shadowed her nights from the moment she met him. She pushed herself away to study his face, suffused as she was with contentment and love. She took his hand and moved it in circles across her rounding stomach. She saw tears in his eyes, and together they began to build the bridge that would span the gulf that had separated them from the first.

"Love me here and now," he whispered, making room for her in the bed, hiding the burning pain at his side beneath his need for her.

"Your wound, darling."

"God help me, I can't wait. I've wanted you all my life," he pleaded.

He needs me. He wants me. That was all Colby's heart heard, and they began undressing each other with swift, demanding fingers, his lips seeking out her breasts, losing himself in their perfectly rounded softness, a thirsty man slaking a long, terrible need.

Colby's nipples and body wakened at his touch, and she followed his command, mounting him. They laughed like loons as they tried to accommodate his wound, devouring and rejoicing together in the oneness that they knew the act of love would give them.

It would be the first time they truly gave of themselves.

Panaman stormed around the trees and bushes surrounding his lair, cursing himself for the near defeat and disaster of the morning. He should have killed Browning and Pierce on the first shots. What was happening to him? Was he going soft? He could not take pleasure in escaping fourteen men who had come after him. He could not take satisfaction that he had faced and escaped certain death at Shad's hands. As he saw it, his old enemy had disdain for him and thought himself the better man for having taken him unawares. His homicidal frenzy at not having killed any of his pursuers frightened the birds out of the trees and every creature in the darkness surrounding him took flight.

At last, fatigued and unable to think of a new murderous scheme, Panaman retreated to his den to lose himself in drink. He felt in his bones that the next few days would see the end of the Brownings and Mannerings, and then he could leave the country. But first he meant to test his carpenter's disguise and get closer to Brawleigh. Never again would he permit Nevil

Browning and his henchmen to get as close as they had that day.

He had no fresh ideas, but he trusted his luck, knowing something would arise to bring his battle to a successful conclusion.

Chapter 43

Colby lay next to Nevil, studying the long, thin face that was even more startling in repose. The vellum-colored skin was stretched taut over fine bones, and his lips, full and beautifully defined, were all that one wanted in a man. She smiled to herself. How well her body knew that.

For a man who should have been laid low after the encounter with Panaman, Nevil had been a stallion, and her body resonated thrillingly from the night's encounters. He had been in fear of hurting the baby, but she assured him he needn't worry. His consideration was another proof of his specialness.

Colby could not credit the evidence of her mind and womanhood. Nevil Browning loved her as much as she loved him. He had been as miserable and unfulfilled as she herself, but most of all, he forgave unconditionally every uncomfortable moment she had given him, amazingly able to understand the roots of her fierce independence.

"What are you thinking about, you minx?" Nevil said, his eyes closed, smiling as his knowing hands sought her out.

"Rest, my darling," she murmured, coming into his good side. "Dr. Lawrence won't think me the best nurse when he sees this bed and imagines what we've been doing here." She touched his bandages and screamed when she saw the stain that had seeped through it. "There's fresh blood there." Colby could hardly breathe with the shock. "The doctor and your mother will kill me."

"What a way to die," Nevil said, pulling her nearer.

Nevil divided his time getting to know his wife and conferring with Tarn, John Lear, and the strange men who came and went all day.

He had never been happier in his life. He couldn't keep his eyes or his hands and lips from lovingly roaming over his wife. His mother told Sylvia Rainwriter they should include Augustus Panaman in their prayers for bringing Colby and Nevil together in what was clearly becoming a love story worthy of the poets.

Brawleigh had never been a happier place, and the family flourished in the same way as the house grew more lovely and welcoming under the skilled hands of so many workmen.

When the weather was fair, Colby and Nevil walked arm in arm in the garden, while men dressed as laborers kept silent vigil. But she was not to know that. When she did realize it, she insisted on an explanation.

"Darling, who are those men, and what are you planning?" Colby asked, disappointed once again that she had not been consulted.

"They are some of Tarn's best men, my dear," he said, leading her back to the house. "I have no intention of giving Panaman a clear shot at you or me again."

"I suspected you had something in mind," she said, touching his arm lovingly.

Nevil looked startled, but quickly covered it up. Keeping secrets from his wife was almost too formidable a task, even for him he chortled inwardly.

"Now, how much credit have I gained in your heart?" Nevil asked cryptically.

At once her ears went up in alarm. But she had learned a few new lessons and waited for Nevil to explain himself.

"I share your love of Brawleigh, Colly, really I do, but for the while I'd rather we moved to Moreton," he said gently. "Don't answer now. Think about it."

Nevil had learned a lesson or two himself and was proud of the phrasing of what should have been an order, at least for his purposes. He leaned down and lay his head against her stomach. The idea of being a father captivated him more each day, and at every turn he demonstrated to Colby how much he cherished her and their baby.

"You're a devil, you are, Nevil Browning," Colby said, brushing her hands lightly over his head. "I am only sorry that

I didn't tell you sooner how much I want to be the mistress of Moreton."

"I think that calls for a celebration," he said happily, "but you must allow me to make all the plans."

Within two days the move to the big house on the hill in the distance was accomplished with near military precision.

Panaman paused in his work to watch the procession of carriages, wagons, and carts move snail-like toward Moreton and felt the blood rush out of his head. Only the need to maintain his masquerade kept him from going wild in front of everyone.

He had hidden what was left of his considerable arsenal in strategic places around Brawleigh while he was supposed to be working on the house and had planned his final attack on the family for that night.

In the beginning he had been as happy as his hate-filled mind could be, savoring leisurely the final destruction he was contemplating. But each day he saw Colby and Nevil behaving as consummate lovers had driven him to want to wreak havoc on them before all his weapons were in place.

Once again he thought about all the lies Cortnage had fed him. Time and again he had said that Colby and Browning hated the thought of each other. Hadn't he seen them quarreling with his own eyes? He had no way of knowing what had changed them, but their happiness with each other only underscored the barrenness of his own miserable existence. He couldn't forget the ease with which Colby has ruined the life he had loved dearly, lording it over the unfortunates of the neighborhood, watching the money he stole from Moreton mounting each year. How often he talked to Cortnage about emigrating to Australia and living the life of a man of property in the colony. And the bitch had robbed him of all this and the brilliant future he felt he had earned.

Chapter 44

The party to welcome Colby as chatelaine of Moreton was the talk of the district, and many of the local dignitaries were put out that Nevil was making it a family affair. At his direction, the family was told to dress in their best finery, and Moreton's farms and cellars were scoured for the best in food and drink. John Lear, who seldom left Moreton since Nevil's return from France, was sent to London posthaste to bring exotic viands back along with jewels from the Browning family vaults.

It was to be a party that few of them would forget.

Colby and her mother-in-law were delighted to learn that Nevil had thought to hire several bagpipers, who came down from London to provide the music during dinner. Wives of some of the local men who worked on Brawleigh were hired to augment the kitchen staff, and the details of the party were heard in the best and meanest houses throughout the area.

Nevil added a fresh twist to divert his guests. He had arranged for several artists to sketch the family in and around the house that day and especially at dinner.

"This is not to be a re-creation of the Last Supper," he told them at tea, risking an accusation of heresy, "but I would like my child to see what we all looked like on the day my darling Colby agreed to preside at my table."

Lear returned to Moreton several hours before the dinner party, laden with jewels and secretive about other things he'd brought back from London. After delivering Lady Miriam's jewel cases, he came into the morning room with a package for Colby.

"We haven't had much time together," Colby noted regretfully. "Maybe when we are all in London again in a few months you and I can go to the shops and galleries as we once did."

Lear walked around the room restlessly, so unlike his usual near-phlegmatic self.

"What's wrong, John? Is something troubling you?"

"Nothing, really," he said too quickly. "I am over the moon that you and his lordship are so happy, and Matthew is doing so well. Even that odd man, Pierce, says I am not quite the fool he thought I was."

Colby knew that John Lear had insisted on being included in the hunt for Panaman and had acquitted himself well.

"I am going away, Colby," he said, sitting down and taking her hand. "Lord Nevil has been kind enough to recommend me to a friend in America, and I am to be trained for business. I've come to like money."

Colby was delighted for him, but sorry for herself, and told him so.

"You were my first and only friend in London. What am I going to do without you?"

"You have your husband, and I know for myself he is the best of men." Lear took her hand and lingered over it. She had never been blind to Lear's feelings for her and from the first had been aware of his growing attraction. Once or twice, in the depths of her unhappiness before her wedding and on her return from Paris, she had almost leaned too close to the comfort of his silent ardor. She owed him much, but she cold never repay him in the way that would have meant everything to him. Her considerable talent for love was given once, and then only to one man.

Colby stood up and put her arms lightly around him.

"I brought you some presents from London," he said, kissing her on the cheek. "They are in your room."

Lear's presents were her London and Paris wardrobes that Nevil had brought back on his yacht. Clothes could never loom large to her, but this was one night she wanted to look her best for Nevil.

Shortly before eight he came into her room carrying a larger jewel case than the one John Lear had given her. He looked splendid in his faultlessly tailored evening clothes. She couldn't help but stare and marvel at her luck in having such a startlingly handsome and loving husband at last.

Nevil couldn't believe how lovely she looked, for he was that rare man who, even in his salad days, thought women were at their most beautiful when they were increasing.

Colby was enchanting in a white gros de Naples round dress with a corsage of pearls and satin outlining her bosom. It pleased him greatly that she was showing unmistakable signs of her condition. The last time he had admired her from afar wearing the same gown was at a party in Paris when they were barely speaking to each other. She had outshone every woman, and he had wanted to tell her so but had been afraid of one of her famous snubs. Now he indulged himself and admired her to his heart's content.

There was a slight difference in the way Colby looked tonight, he noted merrily. The broad white satin sash disposed in folds around her waist showed a slight thickening. He was shrewd enough not to mention the alteration. He was learning quickly and was proud of his new diplomacy.

To him Colby would always be the lithe, black-haired ravishing woman with the grace and look of a panther, the one who scared him half to death by her ill-concealed contempt and caused his head and tongue to run away with him the morning after the famous mill. He had often cursed that day, but not recently. Definitely not these past nights when Colby came into his arms as willingly and wonderfully as he had never dared dream would happen.

Colby couldn't know what was going on in her husband's mind, but she read his eyes and saw there everything a woman needed to feel loved and desired.

Nevil came to her and began fastening a diamond and sapphire necklace around her throat. This time Colby accepted the jeweled masterpiece without demur.

"Do you feel at last that you have the right to wear these?" he asked, bending to kiss the nape of her neck.

Colby leaned back, melting against him.

"Yes."

Together they descended the magnificent winged staircase that commanded the large entry hall of Moreton and made it a showplace.

Lady Miriam, standing next to Tarn, watched them, each thinking Colby and Nevil were everything that aristocrats should look like but seldom did.

Lady Miriam wished that her husband, daughter, and Robert were alive to share the happiness Nevil had found after the arid, lost time following the wounds of Badajoz that had assailed him far too long. The last years of my life will be my best, she thought, and felt a great peace take over her heart.

"We have a surprise for you," the old lady announced, and out of a side door came Lady Barbara Maitland, beautifully gowned in blue, her favorite color, walking majestically with her stick.

Just as she was greeting her, Colby spied an odd exchange of agitated glances between the husbands. The distress on their faces alerted her to an atmosphere of unusual tension between them, and she meant to get to the bottom of it after a warm welcome for their unexpected guest.

As the women hugged each other, Colby heard Tarn say sotto voce, "I hadn't a clue."

They walked off looking worried, and for the life of her Colby couldn't understand what had suddenly transpired to alter Nevil's mood. In their room he had been everything that was benign and casual. She didn't like the change in him at all.

They gathered at last in the blue-and-white drawing room, dominated at both ends by Adams fireplaces aroar with huge logs. Matthew, now that Dr. Lawrence had left, was recuperating so quickly that he was allowed downstairs, although now that she thought about it, Nevil and Tarn had both been difficult and expressed fears that the dinner would be too tiring for him. They'd been loudly overruled, and here he was in an old evening suit of her father's that Ilene and Colby had cut down for him.

Mark, who had never seen such a plush gathering, was everywhere, with John Lear cautioning him to stay close to Matthew.

Nevil was most particular about where everyone was to sit

at dinner and went over the order several times before dinner, which again aroused Colby's suspicions. If she wasn't mistaken, Nevil and Tarn seemed inordinately concerned by what she considered trivialities, and John Lear was sweating although the house was overwarm.

Nevertheless, toasts were given over quantities of champagne until four pipers, handsome in their kilts, arrived to lead the company into the white-and-gold dining room lit with numerous candles, the heavy drapes pulled back, revealing the wide, immaculate lawns lovingly touched by moonlight.

Colby surveyed the long, gleaming table, the Baccarat glass and ornaments, Sèvres china, and a heavy silver epergne laden with luscious grapes, nuts, and other dainties, unable to accept so easily that she was mistress of all this magnificence. She was overawed, wondering how long it would take her to learn to live easily with such splendor.

More servants than she thought necessary dodged the pipers in their never-ending circling of the table, while the wondrous room rang with talk and laughter. She followed the rules religiously, talking during one course to Lear, who was seated on her left, and Tarn, on her right. Colby wasn't at all sure that she would want such formality at every meal and would have to ask Nevil about that when they were alone. Having existed for so long cheese paring and making every penny count for five, Colby was cheerfully overset, but not so hidebound any longer that she could not adjust to this new life.

"Doesn't she look like she has lived here all her life?" Nevil asked, smiling lovingly at Colby.

"I am ashamed, but I must admit Moreton is everything I had heard," she replied, eyes glowing. "I love it."

"Traitor," Matthew and Mark hooted good-naturedly.

"I'm not taking anything away from Brawleigh," she said quickly, "but until you are grown, Moreton is our home, isn't that right, Nevil?"

How the mighty have fallen, her husband thought and laughed delightedly. Whatever Colby did she did with a full and generous heart. He still couldn't believe his good fortune. She was all that he could have asked for in a woman, and more. If only Panaman were safely out of the way, he would ask nothing more of life.

The dinner was drawing to a close, a howling success, and Colby started to tell Nevil so when the chandelier rocked madly and all hell seemed to break loose with a deadly volley of bullets.

"It's come, Tarn," she heard Nevil shout as he and Maitland leaped from their chairs, guns drawn. In a split second she found herself none too gently wrestled to the ground by a piper and pushed under the table with Barbara, her aunt, and Lady Miriam beside her, and the boys a few feet away, placed there by the other burly pipers.

Colby, with her customary impatience to be in the midst of things, tried several times to wrench away from the huge piper, but he held her in a death grip. She'd more than met her match.

"You'll go nowhere, lassie," the man was saying. "Master said to sit on you if it was necessary."

No one doubted that the Scotsman would do just as he was told, and they laughed nervously at the picture of him doing so.

"I like a rousing end to a dinner party as much as anyone, but this is ridiculous," Colby said, trying to keep them all from panicking.

Lady Barbara added, "What a unique way you have of serving dessert, Colby dear!"

As time went by their little sallies dried up, and they listened in alarm to the rising voices on the lawn.

"Everyone up," Nevil shouted, hurrying into the room at last, his face wreathed in smiles, his clothes blood-spattered as he helped the women to their feet.

"It was Panaman, wasn't it?" Colby said, beginning to run outside to see what had happened.

Nevil swung her around and pulled her to him. "We are free of him, my darling. Free."

Lady Miriam was incensed and wanted to know what had been happening. Waiting for her son's return, she had concluded that the dinner party was a ruse to lure the madman into the open, and said so.

"What right had you to put us all in this danger," she said, including Maitland and Lear in her scorn as they came through the door.

Nevil and Tarn tried to talk at once, their guilt written large on their faces.

"We had no choice," Nevil managed to get in first. "He killed a carpenter, left him naked, and was probably working at Brawleigh waiting for the right time to strike."

"Nothing would stop him," Lear broke in. "He killed the old witch, and she never did any harm to him."

"Dear Lady Miriam, you were always in danger from Panaman, but oddly less so at dinner tonight," Maitland said, taking her hand and leading her toward the drawing room. He winked at Nevil over her head and set himself to charm the old lady.

Colby, who had never feared for herself, had already deduced that all the extra servants and the bagpipers were in fact hired to protect the company.

She looked up at Nevil and saw lines of weariness and tension that she hadn't wanted to see before. He had gone to Olympic lengths to keep them safe, but it was a gamble that had taken its toll. She took his hand and brought it to her lips.

"Mama is right," he said, holding her against him. "If Tarn's men had not surrounded the house and brought Panaman down, if his men hadn't moved so fast to get you out of the line of fire, you might have been killed."

She sat down and bade Nevil to sit beside her. She cradled his head against her breasts much as she would the baby that was growing inside her.

"Panaman's dead, and we are alive. Nothing else matters."

And Nevil said, "Amen!"

Epilogue

Now when Lady Colby Browning rides through Moreton village on her great stallion, Midnight, forelocks are pulled, ladies curtsy, and the gentry wave at her enthusiastically. For didn't she keep her promises? A young, qualified doctor, a new steeple for the church, a large school for all the children, and Moreton and Brawleigh ring with parties, picnics, and balls.